Fantasies from the "Frame"
and
Stories off the Stone

ACKNOWLEDGEMENTS

To all those who stroked the keys, cast and fingered the sorts, nailed the plates, and read the words, at Richard Clay's, Bungay, when such scenes as herein could well have been contrived to have taken place:

To Marian, and my old mate Frank Crowley, whose encouragement and patience I have leant upon to complete the task,

and finally:

To all the 'Originators' of today and yesterday, whose identity to our own Industry, shall never be forgotten:

My thanks and best wishes,

Dave Gladwell

Fantasies from the "Frame"

and Stories off the Stone

***

*Stories of printing workers,
and a few simple country folk,
who, perhaps, were not quite so simple
after all when it came to dealing with those
dreadful people from 'away'.*

by Dave Gladwell

Set against a background of the years 1960-1980
in the letterpress and hot-metal composing era
of the Printing Industry

MAYHEM PUBLISHING

First published 1998 in Great Britain by
Mayhem Publishing
(David C. Gladwell), 5 Martin Road, Diss, Norfolk IP22 3HR
All rights reserved

ISBN 0 9532178 0 9

Printed and bound in Great Britain by
Page Bros., Mile Cross Lane, Norwich NR6 6SA

Cover colour separations sets from an oil painting by the Author,
PDQ Reprographics, Broad Street, Bungay, Suffolk NR35 1EF

CONTENTS

1.	Meeting Our Man	7
2.	Out of this World	15
3.	Bully for You ?	25
4.	A Uniform Sort of Story	37
5.	Stable Stuff	47
6.	The Seat of the Problem	55
7.	A Tall Story ?	63
	The Interlude	69
7.	(Again) Antics and Adversity	75
8.	Of Mice and Men	85
9.	A Bit of a Plant	95
10.	Flights of Fancy	101
11.	The Mug Shot	107
12.	May-bee ?	113
13.	"Romance"	121
14.	Away Days	127
15.	A Sticky Customer	137
16.	Turning a Blind Eye	143
	The Epitaph	151
	Glossary of Terms	155-160

Insertions:

A Printer's Lament	36
Depression	62
The Compositor's Colic	94
Tools Illustration	100
Pursestring People	142

PRINT June, 1969

By courtesy of The Graphical Paper & Media Union

PRINT December, 1969

W...

You can go further and far better.

Skilled printers, earn good money in country. So why move out to East Anglia ?

It's true that the good money you'll earn at Clowes' centres in Beccles, Great Yarmouth or Co... may be a little further than in the big towns. True, too, you could be in pocket by selling a house in a high-cost area and buying another — and maybe better — house in Norfolk, Suffolk or Essex where prices are still comparatively reasonable. Or, you could rent a Clowes' house at moderate cost. We also give generous assistance with removal expenses if necessary.

Your biggest gains, though, won't be just materialistic. Whatever you want for yourself and your family — sea, sun, fishing, football, sailing, entertainments, peace and quiet — you'll find all these, close at hand, in East Anglia.

If it's improved quality of life you're after, Clowes' country is the place to make for.

CHAPTER ONE

Meeting Our Men

It wasn't youthful exuberance that perpetuated the telling of fantastic tales, neither could it be said it was wholly the voice of experience. Anyone who could truthfully boast of such a wealth of information as issued by Robin Gray - alias Garbo - would be truly in a class of their own . . . but then so could be the Australian, Yorkshireman, Cockney and many of those who wandered to Dungate to saunter round the stone and fiddle on the frame.

Perhaps then this very unusual character, is to be put in a class of his very own. To be sure, that is what he would have wanted for himself. No, demanded it!

Looking at the appearance would not necessarily lead one to this conclusion. For the era that it was, he would not, for an ageing man, stand out in a crowd. Apart from his personal body odour, people did actually find our friend a very attractive character in many ways. To the 'interloper', he represented much of what the new countryside was all about. Unknown quantities and small surprises around every corner. Mysteries to the 'newcomers' that were easy, everyday events to Garbo, became amusing to many a local person. Unchanged aspects frozen in time, or adventures of a war, after all, not that long ago.

The dingy brown waistcoat, with its crumpled silk back, worn daily over a dark dull shirt, was frayed more than a little by the passage of time. More noticeably a disgustingly generous amount of fine cigarette ash had become engrained as part of the well-worn, well-used look.

This very individual piece of pocketed clothing was a beloved hallmark and a veritable antique displayed in its own lifetime.

Each of the thin cigarettes which hourly had been painstakingly puffed away, and contributed to the familiar markings, had been rolled by the not so steady hand, and grudgingly ran across the thin hard lips. The end slightly soggy, and the smoke a sweet smelling blue from the flake he 'ready rubbed' himself.

Those same dry lips which vented the fertile mind, encircled what at one time, would have been a full set of unstained and unchipped teeth in days of past prime.

Of course, such minor items as teeth and a 'roll-up', could not stand alone in the wonderful world of our unusual friend.

As every lily is pure and delicate, so too in his hands was each of his created tobacco wonders. How much effort went into the individual construction, or how much just stemmed from the ever creative mind on spec, was more than the likes of any human mortal, could assess, or more than an average Cockney could believe! Only can one be sure, that to all of the most mundane things, there was more than met the average eye.

To roll a cigarette, one could easily purchase for a matter of a few pence, a small machine to perform the operation satisfactorily. For Garbo, as nicknamed, this presented a challenge, and by shaping a small piece of cane, affixing it to a fragment of rubber, lovingly cut with expertise from a discarded cycle inner tube, a new article of originality to the world was born.

The contrivance was an effective mixture of ingenuity and eccentric elegance. The cute, canny roller worked to perfection. It became a popular article, freely distributed with typical generosity, to all his colleagues on the vast floor of the Composing Room. Compositors all, and gentlemen of the Press.

Perhaps it was inspired by the time honoured element of Craftsmanship, which, in spite of incentive schemes, could not be extinguished by greed in every heart. Or was it in fact, like many of his tales, herein, one mind's way to keep its sanity within the walls of industry's depressing gloom.

So, no fool was this memorable man. In very many ways an extremely wise one. His boast of never having visited a dentist could be believed form the acrid smell of breath. It held an intensity that would give great grace to any farting dog. To look at the gappy teeth one would immediately conclude a visit to the tooth doctor was long overdue, but it was most unlikely.

Garbo preferred his own treatment and surgery, and not exclusively within the confines of his own home. Firstly, to readily rub a generous quantity of whisky on the offending tooth's gum. Secondly, to hold an even larger quantity, neat, in the mouth for one minute.

'Not a second longer', the oracle emphasised, craggy bent forefinger raised singly in caution. Then following a quick swallow, a long-nosed pair of pliers should be set to the tooth and the offensive article was suitably extracted from the galant gums, with an artistic twist of the wrist.

To say that most of the teeth were probably loose in the gums anyway, would be a fair point, but not one acceptable from our wholly loquacious and genuine Friend's personal point of view.

It appeared however, the only reasonable excuse for all of those who were too frightened or faint hearted to try the recommended remedy themselves. Foreigners they might be, but they were not totally stupid! Saving the local Dentist's fee was small compensation in the light of agonies imagined for abortive or even successful efforts. Excruciating pain and the likely consumption of more than enough whisky were only the bonuses.

It was just accepted as the normal situation, when, from time to time, another cavernous black hole was proudly exhibited.

If ever anyone thought they were going to get away with less than about ten minutes from any of Garbo's tales, they were definitely in for a disappointment, each unique episode appeared tuned to perfection.

It mattered not that the Bonus Scheme worked out at one pence per minute saved. Many constantly found themselves assessing the price of a yarn after four or five minutes in a fit of despondency. Afraid to disagree, or even slightly question for fear of further elaboration or extension, it became the fashion to incredulously agree or maintain a very discreet and prudent silence.

Our Man would very predictably position himself in the most awkward of, and obstructive, impassable, inaccessible postures, deliberately whereby to prevent the luckless recipient from escape or progressing with his immediate task. Indeed, many found that only outright rudeness would disenchant the visitor and result in at least one quiet week. Garbo would return, and this was the sixties when people had time for themselves and each other still, not even the Credit Card had arrived.

The unfortunate fellow who had the great burden of permanently working in the next frame had cultivated, over the years, a very clever grunt which could be taken as affirmative or negative, yet, denied as meaning either. It was a relief for him when others suffered, and he eventually confessed that the perpetual drone passed through one ear and out the other. Only the most extraordinary epistles would momentarily deter him. This success poor Perky put down to wild wartime experiences of being trapped in submarines for weeks on end, unable to escape from some most unattractive companions to arms in the King's Royal Navy.

On many occasions it could well fall the lot of the one whose ears had become burdened, to be the subject of much mirth within the Composing room. As the lined face related incidents with an expression befitted to the saga in seriousness, behind and above his shoulder, would appear some individual, or individuals, set upon the idea of getting the listener to laugh or smile. Poor Garbo would become quite perplexed at how on earth anyone could ever be smiling at the tale of perhaps wonderous woe or incredulity he was relating!

This was not to be the case for the introduction of the newly arrived Cockney, eager to learn the wiles and wary ways of the East Anglian Countryside, to which he came to work, in the wonderful world of make believe, in the prized printing works of dreaded Dungate.

Garbo's great day of the year was the annual trip to the Norfolk County Show and coincided with his immensely active mind and interests. Upon his return there were always tales. Today was to be no exception, but these were tailored to an abridged edition for the Cockney's eventual humiliation. Garbo had become tired of the Interloper's caustic charade with the piece of grass in his mouth and the acted out accent.

'How yew a gittin along tew day then, old Master?' came the corrupted question.

'Not as good as yesterday, when I saw all manner of interesting things and genuine people,' Garbo responded.

'Especially the bacon pigs,' he said craftily with his eyes narrowing in evil intent.

'Really. Are they a special type of pig then?' enquired the inquisitive Cockney, flicking back yet again his long dark greased hair.

'Yes, boy, they are. Especially the old streaky bacon ones,' the answer was provided.

'What do something different for all them do they?' queried the streetwise sinner.

'That they do. Give them a special sort of dietary control,' Garbo responded holding his gaze steady.

'See, to get the bacon streaky, proper like. They feed them, then they starves them, feed them and starve them. That's what does the job. Bit like the rings on a tree trunk.' His lined face did not crack an inch.

'How very interesting. I didn't know that,' the gullible chunky built, thirty-year old Cockney commented.

The dour proofing press man grinned to himself.

'Yes but not quite as interesting as the single sucker milking attachments on the dairy cows though,' Garbo continued, intent on wreaking his revenge for the dialect slights. There were a few smiles from the Local Lads as he drew the inevitable intrigue of enquiry.

'Single sucker eh. What's that then?' Cockney asked.

Garbo permitted himself the edge of a smile for his luckless listener's ignorance.

'Well, you see. It's a sort of labour saving device. New technological innovation. Whereas the milkmaid used to have to pull four teats to get the milk they now cut three off and a tube comes out just one. Very clever idea, popular with the girls.'

The leg pull was complete as the Cockney was clearly taken in and appeared both impressed and convinced.

The brown bearded Aussie uttered just one of his regular words, 'Arsehole', and carried on working .

There were several smiles in the composing room and it would be several months before the New Arrival would realise he had been well and truly set up.

Of such was Garbo's mind. Nobody could be just too sure what element of truth laid behind his claims. Perhaps many were contrived as a form of industrial action, to halt advance in Garbo's own rebellious stand against the march of progress, production and profit.

The gathering of men, bound together in their closed shop, and restrictive practices of centuries past, were just the same as many a *Chapel* in other printing houses, large or small, with a mass of very odd bods and sods.

The religious connotation of the name meant little, but the foundation by Caxton in the Westminster Church implied much to the perpetuation of the name.

Before the Union came to pass, no doubt Gutenburg, with the first creation of moveable type, was as proud of his skills as these craftsmen were, and guarded his inky secrets of the mirror imaged word just as jealously as these did today. Before him the monks who were illustrators of the ornate Initial letter at the start of chapters, professed their expertise in an adorative modesty to their God. The Print Union SLADE claimed it was their birthplace and birthright. The NGA, in its male discriminative elitism, skill and pride, thought otherwise and ruled the roost in the composing rooms.

These two exclusive clubs, solely derived from poorly paid apprenticeships, produced eccentrics by the dozen. Skill and experience came by travelling between printing firms, but our dear Dungate, like many other book houses, had been very much isolated from this until its expansion. It suffered, largely in silence, the slings and arrows of outrageous 'misfortune', the increased presence the nasty NGA brought with it. There were however tremendous advantages as wages and profits soared with profit sharing generously distributed.

These were however happier days, when comradeship bore out the true historical value of the alternative word to the Chapel, it was - *'The Companionship'*.

Garbo resented all forms of modern change, and 'the interlopers', but nothing as much as the incentive bonus scheme. He was, if nothing else, a prophet and popular relief from the bore of the black and the white.

Meanwhile the productivity rolled. Great machines spewed sheets of print on paper from their mighty moving iron beds and cylinders. Letters laid in cases. Proofs paraded upon frames. Page upon page slept stacked in piles, awaiting their wakening to produce book after book. Some were encyclopaedias, others dictionaries, but none of them contained the volume to compare with Garbo's creative mind.

CHAPTER TWO

Out of this World

Invariably people always remembered best, their first experience with Garbo. One of the newer arrivals had a particular expertise with things metal and mechanical. Any contraption from a waterproof watch to a Rolls Royce was fair game for his fickle fingers.

Garbo accepted this talent and greatly respected it. He was himself a very handy bloke with anything functional and always interested. This threw up some cruel common ground for the person to be introduced to Garbo's world of the Wireless, and of course, an audience was required too!

Amidst Garbo's ingenious inventions and heinous handicrafts, there was one permanently on display in his front room. This exhibited masterpiece had been conveyed to work in a box for the room's worshipful approval, and the mechanical expert's interest.

The crystal set in the box had utilised only the most basic of materials but it really did work. It was a success and tribute to his immense ingenuity and greatly admired by all and sundry.

The first signs of disaster emerged when in an unguarded moment some unfortunate individual asked if he had ever done any thing like it before.

A great grin spread from one hair-ridden ear to the other. It was now too late for escape. He positioned himself and trenched in for a tale.

'Why, yes. Didn't I ever tell you about it then?' he began benignly

'Must have been a few years ago now, shortly after the second world war. When things were still a bit hard to get hold of. Hun, he got a lot to answer for still.'

'Went along to the Misses' jumble sale she was a running for the Church. Stood around a bit in case there was trouble with people scrapping over the clothes, et, cet. terra, ha ha! Now there is now't as strange as folk when there's a bargain about.'

'Getting a bit fed up with it all, I wanders along to the bric-a-brac. See the knick-knacks displayed in a muddle on the table. Search to see if there is anything of use or interest for me like.'

'Well, blast boy, under a pile of old comics I find something alright. Real little treasure. Set of earphones, from a blinking Spitfire pilot's headgear.'

'More scrabbing around under the shoes and there is an old receiving set too. Offers half a crown for them, which is very acceptable in those days, I might add, and off I goes with my new treasures.'

'Well, nearly off, that is. Last stall by the door is the village bobby. Blasted nuisance the man is, always poking about somewhere. Load of rubbish on his stall there is, but I think about the pheasant's on the marshes and want to keep the peace. Of course, got me hands full I have, but a shilling is in me fingers still which I

16

was going to give to the Chapel. Put it in their box on the way out.'

'Drop it down on the table I do and say to him, with authority like, that's what them sort of people are used to, "Find me something for that then Officer, please".'

'He lean over, down behind the table, and come up smiling with a bit of blooming head gear in his hands. Sets a real dusty old bowler hat on my head, and the blighter pulls it down right hard to me ears. Blast, I'm something riled and can hardly see. Cock me head and creeps off home feeling and looking a proper Charlie. What else can I do I ask you, with my hands full.'

'Settled down back at home, articles in the shed, I pick up a bit of wood to make a few sticks for the fire, when I has a rare good idea come upon me.'

'Back off to the shed, my workshop, I goes, and out come all the odds and ends kept in an old mahogany box me father gave me. Lovely bit of wood with dovetail joints.'

Norman knowingly interjected, 'Craftsman made of course!' He knew that line off by heart.

'You've got it,' said Garbo appreciatively. 'Down I get's me head and off to work we are, real keen like. Apart from me meals, spends almost the whole weekend in there. Wife she say a me, "What a you a doin' of in there boi?" I keep her in the dark like.'

'Until Sunday evening that is. Time come when we usually bikes into town together to have a look in the shop windows, have a walk round. Jar in a respectable tavern and a mither or two with friends few but of considerable quality. Imagine her surprise when in my best suit I disappears into the workshop; and then comes out with a hat on my head. Yes! The bowler hat!'

'She say to me that is the rummest place she ever known a person to keep a brand new hat. Can hardly believe her eyes and ears when I tell her it's the one from the jumble sale. She a thinks it look as though I've a given the earth for it. I just keep on smiling.'

'Bit special though I feel tonight. "Right, Gal, were going to have a rare little outing tonight," I say to her. "We're a going into Town on the bus." Wife she's a something excited about that.'

'I tell you, master, we've crossed that blasted Dam so many times, I guess we know every darn tree, bush, puddle and stone, personally and off by heart. Today, sat upstairs on the top deck it don't look one tiny scrap different.'

'I takes off the bowler hat and shows her what's inside. She can barely contain her excitement and amazement. Mind you, I feel she has good reason.'

'There, reduced down, and attached to the lining is one of the headphones, surrounded by a few neatly secured wires. Make a tiny connection I do with a very small screwdriver I have brought along in my top pocket, and there it is.'

The very familiar pause announcing that the apex of the adventure was nigh, was expertly executed.

'Clear as a bell is the radio. Light Programme, if I'm not mistaken. Music coming in loud and clear. Turn it down a bit I do so as not to attract too much attention like, from the other people as is sat upstairs with us.'

'Place the hat on her little old head and she wears it and listens in, all of the rest of the way into town something pleased and intrigued.'

'Off the bus first, soon as we arrive, been waiting to disembark with a nifty step I have. Help the wife off with a strong arm. Now, afore we enter the good tavern, I stand in a shop doorway at the top of the hill. That's what I was looking for. A bit of high ground.'

'Bless my soul, a tiny movement of the winder set against the small watch face and the programme changes. It's New York and the World Service News! How about that then?' he concluded with great pride.

A very dry voiced patient Percy made one his of most unusual interjections. 'Thought you was going to say it was Radio *Man-hat-on*,' he said.

Nobody ever had as good a repeat performance of that particular tale again. One word had ruined it!

Arriving at work next day our Dear dour friend made some sort of a diabiolical disaster in dismounting from the trusty steed of a cycle and attracted a little attention. It was observed by everyone that he walked with a limp into work to curse and clock on.

One or two unsuspectingly enquired of his health. Of course it could not be anything normal, and in no time at all they found themselves manipulated into the front line of an unusual event.

'We all get bad backs at times,' Garbo said, 'but I'll warrant there will be none of you with a cause for it like I have got today.'

'Getting along home from work I was last night, and arrive up there by Tunny's Corner. Along come this darn great lorry. Right massive noisy fellow it was, one of those with the ten wheels set on it.'

'Blowed if just as he get close to me, too darned close, I'm aware of something a flying through the air towards me. Running me bike up on the pavement I find myself parallel with a garden wall. Thrusting myself forward and pressing down on the handlebars my body leave the bike in a position similar to that of a high jumping athlete performing the Californian roll. Force myself into the position I do. By the grace of God, or the luck of the Devil, don't ask me which, I just make it over the flint wall in time to hear a resounding thud on the pavement.'

'At first I'm not sure whether it's the spikes from the gooseberry bush sticking into my back, or what on earth I has done. Whatever it is believe me it's painful!'

'Later I realise that there was a very slight rub as I passed horizontal over the wall, and there is the sufferance of an abraised back and a slightly twisted spine. Blasted thing's still sore this morning as you see.'

'Still it's an ill wind that blows no good. When I gets back over the wall, out of the unfortunate person's garden, the ruddy lorry has disappeared from sight. Surprise, surprise, though, what should I find?'

Everyone wondered, the possibilities were eternally endless. Not another dead body surely?

'Blast it's a two-hundred weight sack of spuds. Cor, hence the thud that would have squashed me flat had it not been for my lightening reactions.'

'Right, master, there's no one will help those, who do not help themselves. Couple of strong quick movements and the sack is on my toe of the left foot. Quick twist and a flick and the sack is sitting on me handlebars and home we goes.'

'Suppose I got me money's worth for a bit of a bad back though.'

The crass stupidity of man has often to be seen to be believed. Someone actually said, 'Not one of your better days then.' Moans meandered around the anguished audience.

They denied later it was a question. Claimed it was a comment, at worst only a statement. Whatever, it was enough. More than enough, to produce a double dose.

'A good day is one spent out in the open, like I will on Sunday when I goes an angling,' said Garbo. Now they all knew they were really in for it.

Every fine fisherman has his day, and every angler renowned for the tales he tells. Garbo as one can imagine, was no exception to the rule. Pike were amongst his favourite of quarries.

Quite frequently the average angler would have difficulty in catching livebait to order. Not so Garbo. He claimed to have plumbed into an underground stream and utilised the drainage system. Thereby he had created a subterranean livebait chamber which could be raised up in provision as and when required. Too complicated to just keep them in a pond of course, like anyone else would have done.

The artificial lures he constructed, often in work's time, were truly excellent. Superbly balanced and realistic, each one was a work of art. No doubt they were partially responsible for the amazing results he claimed to have. It was quite often that these ingenious inventions were introduced into alleged tales of capture we thought he did not have, not even on a good day!

A few Zander had been introduced sixty miles away to the river system. Within days his claim to fame was not one of these, oh no. Garbo's catch was the original very rare crossed hybrid between a perch and a pike itself. It surpassed the biggest caught to date, but unfortunately no proof existed, the luckless fish having been consumed that very evening by the hungry Grey family satisfyingly smelted into some exquisite cuisine

The most notable catch was his giant eel. Surprisingly enough this leviathan specimen was not captured by rod, line, bab or trap. Something entirely unusual.

'Damn fine evening it was, been one of those long summer days, warm, close, dry and sunny. Had a long, very long, dry spell for nigh on six weeks. Dreadful drought approaching.'

'Getting up along the straight, pedalling well on the oiled machine, my attention is attracted by what appears to be a dark shape in the gutter at the kerbside.'

'As I get even nearer the shape appears to be moving slowly. I'm forced to believe from its actions it is a giant snake. Be unusual that size for sure. Don't ask me what species I thought it was. I've no ideas in my mind at all. A black snake in these parts? Cannot be.'

'Common thing mind you in my Middle East days, in service of the King. Great ole black things there were out there, sting like a hornet. Lived in the latrines. Couldn't kill you though.'

'Off me saddle steps I with a swing of the leg and a glide to a halt, and peers down.'

'Well, bless my soul if it isn't an old eel. I mean old too by the size of him. Massive thing with only the faintest amount of slime on his strong supple body. Thicker round than my wrist he is.'

'I wonder to myself how in Hell's name he's a got himself there? Nearest river water is half a mile away in a straight line. Even the blasted old pond is a fair way away, must be quarter of a mile. No ditches in the immediate area either.'

'Naturally it come to me that the poor cratter has been dried out of its usual habitat with all the lack of rain. All this darned hot and dry weather we been a having, old boy, he was on a last desperate journey overland in search of water. Got hisself stuck in the kerb with little energy left to raise his head above the pavement. Poor devil.'

'Getting out the old extending metal tape measure I soon confirms it is a damn fine eel. Measures three feet, three inches and three-eighths. Fair tempted to take him home for my dinner, but no, thinks that would not be fair. Not sort of sporting if you know what I mean.'

'So what do I do? Spit on me hand a few times and run it round his head. See his eye shift around towards me. Fix me with a beady sort of stare he do. Wondering in his mind no doubt whether I be friend or foe.'

'Very gently and firmly now, still in silence, together there we are, strangers but friends. I place's a very straight forefinger just down beneath his expanded gills. Lift up the great old head.'

'Blast man he finds a silent surge of energy from somewhere, maybe drawn from the very strength of my hands, who knows? Away he goes across 'cross the pavement, twisting his muscled body, target well set in his crafty mind.'

'Under the hedge and straight across the recently harvested cornfield towards the river. Another friend helped in need I think to myself.'

'Blinkin' marvellous things eels you know. Big travellers. Right up from the Sargasso Sea in their infancy. Set aside in a slippery world of their own.'

Garbo gloated in his sole supremacy, and looked for praise. As there was not any forthcoming he finished off.

'World would be a funny place if a man can't help a friend, be it man or beast!'

Page cords trailing from the skein around his neck, apron flapping at his knees, off stalked Garbo to the Stores, in search of accents, or another victim, tossing a wooden quoin from one hand to the other.

The ever watchful Donny departed from the service hatch at great speed as Garbo's path became sure. The able assistant, reliable Ronnie, ran to the toilets searching for the winner of the 2.30 at Newmarket as keen as Jason in pursuit of the golden fleece.

Chappie the galley gatherer, grumpily hobbled his leg iron to an evacuation area of safe secluded concealment away from prying eyes and organisation. The *Daily Mirror* of the day was not yet completely read, and there was always a nap on his mind if the bleeders would leave him in peace for long enough to drop off for a while.

The dross on the casting pots took the shine off the molton metal, but launched from its liquid life into the pulsating machine it was reborn again, niche and name, Caslon's kern and capital created.

Shiny galleys of newly cast type shimmered on the racks outside the casting room, waiting in their virginity to have their faces skimmed with the ink roller. Launched into the debauched life of the printed word and all its complications from here on, bathed in leisure, learning and legal licence.

CHAPTER THREE

Bully for You?

The rain lashed down and the wind swept it across the open East Anglian terrain driving the droplets into the cyclists' faces, stinging as the pedals were pushed on the way to work.

Soon the small sleepy country town streets would fill with a busy-bee-ness in the early hour of the day as hundreds launched themselves towards the doors of the unwelcoming factory.

The bicycle still ruled supreme as the duly dominant method of travel, the inconvenience of the car had not really arrived for the habit of short journeys.

Soaked Compositors and Keyboard operators trooped dripping through the doors, leaving a wet trail behind them as they stood to queue at the clocking in machine.

Readers shook and exercised their umbrellas dry with a sense of their own importance. Clock cards were inserted and the handle pressed down. The bell pinged done its drastic deed, and punched a hole recording the dreaded presence of the day and time of arrival. The drips from oil-skin capes and raincoats mixed with the wet footprints on the floor to make a darkened pathway, indicating the route to the crowded locker room.

Cramped and crammed in colleagues jostled and smeared each other with a welcoming wetness. Some by a mad moron's minor mistake and mumbled apology, others with a deliberate mischievousness or ill intent as the outer garments were removed.

The long narrow steel doors received their contents and wellingtons were stored at the bottom amidst cussing and clanging as doors were closed.

Some with agility tottered upon one foot doing up shoelaces whereas others made the full body bend down to the floor.

Garbo in the wealth of his wiles and experience, avoided doing either of these, too many times had he seen nudgings to the floor amidst much mirth.

In a stony silence he removed the well-worn ex-army cape, complete with cycle inner tube repair patches, which he claimed had been his companion in amazing adventures, and thrust it into the cabinet.

He knelt down to remove one of the treasured galoshes and wiped it immaculately clean with his handkerchief and placed it on the shelf, before repeating the process for its shiny black blissful partner.

Course now set for the beloved frame, his second home, the eyes gleamed in the anticipation of a recountment contrived to impress.

Arriving at his appointed place, Garbo positioned an antique looking coffee tin precisely on the top of his frame to receive the drips from the roof, then proceeded to mop the wetness from his working surface. No sooner done, than he made the normal announcement for such inclement occasions.

'Rain fall overnight well over the two inches and still a comin' down, there'll be trouble a-foot,' he predicted in general terms to one and all.

It went largely unnoticed so he tried again, never to be put off course completely.

'Reminds me of the great floods when I was a lad,' he called to the dampened dismals of the day completing yesterday's dockets for the bonus department.

Noting that two or three heads were now raised, he interrupted the cunning concentration of fiddling up more pennies in performance premiums for the previous day. He launched himself towards them, speedily seizing the glimmer of an opportunity.

'Blast yes! That was a rare rum year that was. Father he say to me, we should a be getting down to the marshes to see how the cattle were a fairing, and off we go on the horse and cart.'

'Had we a fair might of rain overnight I can tell you. Blinking old Waveney she had burst her banks and poured right out over the marshes.'

'Each of the fields looked like a great old mirror as they stretched out each side of the road we trotted along. Pretty as a picture, can see it now,' Garbo enthused.

Two or three more people joined the audience to delay the start of the depressing day's work and attend the forthcoming lecture.

'Water start to run across the road when we get near the destination. Soon it's up to the horses knees and the wheels of the cart are under the water. Trusty steed, she still a walk on, sure of foot.'

'Me? Sat up by Father, aside him on the cart, feeling something proud to be beside him and included in the proceedings, I can tell you!'

'All of a sudden we see most of the darn cattle found a little ridge of higher ground, and are standing huddled together in a close group. Mooing their old heads off when they see us. No grass to eat, see, all under water. Hungry old devils now. Main purpose of the visit.'

'Big question though. Where is the old black bull?' Garbo's eyes sourly scanned the fatal few assembled endeavouring to stimulate enthusiasm.

'Oh, no! Not another good load of old *bull* is it?' said a disheartened Yorkie.

Garbo dug out the baccy tin, commenced his roll-up, and continued the tale.

'Bull it is my friend!' he stated undeterred.

'My ear, being young, sharp and fresh, hear a bellow on the air and my keen eye scan the field. There he be. About two hundred yards away by the fence up to his great old black bulging chest in water.'

'Father, he's real concerned and say he's afeared of losing the beast. "Lose the beast, lose the job, Boy," he say to me.'

'I can see it's a serious situation in spite of my youth and wonder what can be done. Father he's a beside hisself with the possibilities.'

'Now as it happen the cart is only a couple of foot from the fence. As Father turn round to see where he can drop the first bale of straw for the cattle off, I seizes my opportunity.'

The eyes blazed and Garbo took a step backwards and raised his elbows. Demonstrating with a thrust of his arms into the air, and a quaint quick step forwards, he claimed his stake to fame and fortune.

'I leaps on to the top of the wooden fence and start to tip-toe tight rope along the top rail steady as a rock.

Father shout out to me to come back but I keep straight on in my own set way.'

'Not a lot changed over the years there then,' commented Herbert bathing in the beery breath of a good night at the Old Oak.

'Soon I am half way out to the old black bull and have a plan of action in that young keen mind. Stop and take stock of the situation I do.'

'Old bull is a bellowing at one end of the journey, Old Chap he's a yowling at the other. Undeterred I continue steady and true.'

'Soon I am right at the old bull and tell him to steady down. He look at me a bit quizzical and wade towards me.'

'Reach over, then I do, and start a scratching him between the eyes as his head come towards me in his uncertainty. No one been that near him before by reason of his truly terrifying nature.'

'All of a sudden, friends we are, bull and I. Struck up a damned fine relationship.'

The Bodybuilder interrupted with a knowing smile and quiet helpful comment. 'We *bullieve* you my friend.'

Garbo gleamed in appreciation and continued.

'Soon I had a strong young hand round each ear. At exactly the right moment I launches myself from the fence top and am astride the great beast in position to ride him.'

'I start to pull and twist his ears like you would a steering wheel. Or capstan to the rudder I suppose I should say in the waterborne sense.'

'Old black beast he respond to me, little old boy that I am, and afore long we are swimming across the field towards Father standing there waving his arms. Mind you he is not alone now. About a dozen arrived from the village hoping to cross the road further down but find it impassable. Doctor, decorator, policeman about his duties. Postman trying to get to work, I recall.'

'As I get within a few yards of them all they start to cheer and clap, and I can see the relief on Father's face.'

'Blast do you know what, he put a rope through the ring on his nose and tie him up on dry ground, and then do you know what happened and he go and do?' Garbo questioned the crew of the Composing ship.

'I should think that the old bull has a bloody good shit!' exclaimed the tall tanned Australian with his normal keen and natural sense of crudity.

'Gave you a damned good *bullocking*, I suppose?' said the Cockney.

'Right you are, master! Clip me round the ear and say I got me shoes and socks all wet. Mother will be riled. That's what you call gratitude for you. Very much unappreciative!' he concluded.

Then turning on his heel in the departing strides he threw back the well-aimed comment.

'Like a lot of these bloody people from away!'

'Yeah, they are all wankers, ain't they mate,' said the Northumberland Nerd jogging Yorkie's arm and making the coffee slop on to his grey warehouse coat inducing catcalls and, 'Daft, dopey bastard, look out!!' response.

The day had started. Copy was turned and proofs produced. The bowler spun whipping off tiny tight rolls of soft metal to mitre the angles of a pica rule box.

Heads well down, tweezers poked and pried into the priceless practices of print.

Well some time later on in the day, it can positively be said, it was not the fault of the Cockney that it had befallen to him to be the well appointed corrector of the Author's proofs for *'How to train your Dog'*.

There was a nasty sneaking suspicion that foreman George was more than enjoying his decision where to place the work. Renowned for a very funny sense of Midlands humour, he had probably played with the idea for an hour or so, knowing exactly what such a title would invoke. The Clicker certainly had the edge of a smile on his lips when he said sarcastically, 'Any queries and I expect Garbo will help you out.'

The luckless London lad then read the title!

Upon return to the frame, a gleam shone brightly from the Old Man's eagle eyes. It was more than apparent that the ever-vigilant friend, who never missed anything, had set his mind and soul on imparting some gem of his ephemeral wisdom, drawn from the stock of absolutely inexhaustible experiences.

For some this was likely to be of quaint collector's material indeed but most hardly a brief break from the boredom.

'Funny you should mention about training dogs,' he opened forth enthusiastically.

There was an ominous silence for a few seconds as a general depression settled itself in.

'We didn't!' retorted a somewhat shirty Shrewsbury Shirker, in certain anticipation of what was to come and endeavoured to make an unsuccessful escape.

The wily old framework of bones positioned itself in a strategically impassable position. No mortal living soul could ignore or retreat without being blatantly rude.

Undoubtedly all were 'had', and very obviously would now have to take more medicine for the day. At least this time most had three or four menial start up tasks to perform whilst participating in the role of the absolutely adoring audience, captured in truly rapt wonderment. Garbo launched forth with a winning smile, or was it a likeable leer?

'You know that little old dog I got at home, she's a real sharp 'un. Don't miss a blooming thing!'

'Said to the wife the other night so I did. "You know Gal, this is the best darn dog we ever did have. Good with the gun, fine round the house and likes the grandchildren". See it's all about training you know. Mind you I put a lot of it down to feeding as well.'

'Far too many people over feed their animals. Make fools of them they do. Always treated our dogs like humans we have.'

Kentish Kid, who was well known for his apt remarks, inquired, and half-heartedly stated, 'Tell them stories do you Robin?'

The narrator continued totally unperturbed as though a word had never been spoken.

'Yes, the other night you know, just after tea, Wife had made one of those big apple pies with currants and dates in. You know the sort, the ones you seldom see in shops.'

Never having lunched with him in the confines of his most remarkable residence, nobody knew. However, obviously one could only but lose to disagree, and at least the conversation showed promise not yet having departed from the basics of reality. Well, it all made a welcome break in a boring day of author's corrections one supposed.

'Aha!, do you know, that little old Labrador dog, she was a curled up by the kitchen door minding of her own business. Wife, she was a getting ready the vegetables for tomorrow's lunch. All sorts of goodies in it from the garden. Nothing like the soil of a happy home. Nurtured, manured and respected like a friend to get the best out of it.'

'Crap on his friends he does then,' muttered Yorkie under his hand.

Garbo continued with enthusiasm.

'Had some carrots there. Real good uns. Not too big though. Carrot get too tough if it's as round as your fist at the top. I can grow them that large for the Shows though if I want to. Must say I am fed up with keep on winning the prizes there and gone off it a little. No, these were long and firm with a fine top on them.'

'Turning one in her hand, was the wife, when she noticed a small imperfection. See that it have a touch of termite in it.'

Surprise, surprise, the listeners, could rarely expect any thing but the very essence of correctness from Garbo's garden.

'Truly and *mite-illy* amazing!', rejoined the smirking Arthur down from the stones for sorts.

'Handing it to me she say she don't a think we should be a having of this one. Quite right I agree, better not be a having this one. Toss it over to the dog I do see.'

'It don't quite get exactly straight to her. Didn't want it too near case it startle her. Up she get herself and have a look. Put her head on one side and stare at the carrot. Raise a quizzical eye and look at me.'

Garbo's head enacted the scene quite dramatically.

'Real pretty she is, you know the way Labrador's are. Slow down with the head and very gently get it in her mouth, then, take it back to the door where she was a laying.'

'Right soft mouth she's got that dog. Do you know she can carry a new laid egg from the run and put it down at my feet without even cracking the shell of it, let alone break it. Not only that, she has brought me a partridge's egg before now when we are out walking.'

'Can't get a word in edgeways though,' said Wally.

Nobody knew, or much cared, but they all wished, somewhat wistfully, that Garbo would arrive with an egg of any description in his mouth some days. Perhaps then perchance they should all have a quiet day.

'Gets it *eggs*actly right, eh?' came in the yawning Yorkie.

Back into the entertainment line plunged Garbo.

'Anyway, gets the carrot she do, just like I tell you so, and do you know what that crafty little old beggar done?'

Their minds boggled with the combination of possibilities and impracticalities in the purposeful pause.

'Blow me, she a laid there and peeled that carrot! She peeled that with her teeth as clean as a whistle. Yes Master! She peeled that darn carrot, then she looked at me again seeking my approval afore she ate it.'

'Funny you should say that', said Yorkie. 'We were watching the telly the other evening and our dog sat by the door. I gave it an apple and she peeled that!'

Garbo looked in plain disbelief that he could be outdone by this brash northerner. Such was his silence and open disappointment that the Yorkshire accent added in a *coup de grace* '. . . with a *knife*!' Absorbing the effect he turned away quickly, and hastily resumed activities at some other suitably appointed and distant place.

The Old fellow returned to his frame, momentarily crushed, spat on the floor, ground the emission into the greasy well-worn concrete floor amidst strewn sorts, and snorted more snuff.

Five minutes later, plus a very good blow on the grizzly handkerchief, and behold, flooding back was the versatile and durable Garbo's confidence.

From the area of the sorts cabinet emerged strains from one of the famous War story volumes. Escapades of an unusual nature, even incredulity, from the never ending mine of ingenious information.

Poor old Arnie, at least with the beginnings of senile dementia he would have forgotten he had heard it all before, and, after all, at least he never made a bonus to start with. It was not quite the same waste of money for him. He only came to work to enjoy the companionship of his friends and collect the football pools coupons!

The sorts laid themselves against the brass setting rule in the composing stick, looking up, smirking in their shiny newness and satisfied in their solace and silence.

Quickly combinations of fingered spaces changed places. Justification of yet another the line and moment, as part of, yet preceding posterity.

A Printer's Lament

Above our sold and soiled brain, fluorescent flickers tube,
to light the burdens of our way, forced into numbered cube.
Not as a person, or a soul, a cabbage or a king,
but as a factory worker, a tired, faceless thing.

He was an individual, but then that didn't pay,
to have a number standing out, in such an oddish way.
So he was pushed and pressured, till to standard did conform,
and character inhibited, 'till he was just the 'norm'.

And so with money for his bread, adjust his way of life,
to profit much through greedy thrust, of sharp industrial knife.
Then he shall come, in time, 'tis true, to cast his cares aside,
his Principles will be a thing, that's scattered far and wide.

Skill and pride, a Craft once knew, of printed word we read,
incentive schemes and dirty books have slain completely dead.
The satisfaction of a day, when something whole was made,
a work of art, a masterpiece, its interest now betrayed.

What for this slave, moronic thing, burns at the bitter end?
A life's work done, health all gone, a mind that will not mend?
For if his fifty years have passed, or maybe some before,
they'll toss him on the scrap heap, as some misshapen whore!

CHAPTER FOUR

A Uniform Sort of Story

It is recalled one of Garbo's most legitimate claims to fame and success, borne out by other's real life witness, was that our mutual friend did indeed attain the rank of sergeant in the Army.

The fact that his service unit varied from the guards (when he was on a 'high' someone said), to the infantry, artillery and the redoubtable royal engineers, proved no surprise. Some workers were disappointed it contained no reference to the commandos, even more were amazed that no claim was ever made to serving in the Intelligence Corps or the super-action man role of a performing paratrooper.

However, the colourful range of his epics in these fields were by far the most entertaining to the vast majority of his listeners. Those preferring the country flavoured tale or two, embellished with unusual flowers and creatures were the people *'from away'*. Often invoking insults from colleagues that the 'Townies', were prepared and ready to believe anything about the countryside! In many ways they were correct!

Perhaps to them in their blissful ignorance, they did not appear to be quite so grossly exaggerated, or they were at least, less sure when their humble gullible minds travelled on a journey of fictional fantasy.

Only the realms of a Compositor's work appeared excluded from the easy elaboration process. Perhaps the round niched founder's type of his forefathers held too much foreboding for him. Maybe he thought it would be an insult to the trade he loved?

Brass rules and borders beckoned his skills, chemical compounds became magically mastered in his horny hands. There was even greater expertise in the bread and butter basic rate approach to determining what he considered was a fair day's work in this wild and airy flatland.

Only the teller ever knew whether he was truly taking listeners as fools or, perchance, really believed his yarns himself. Many of his tales were clearly inspired by the truth and the actual point of diversification sometimes easy to see. At times it took no great mind to see the psychological significance of the story. The meat of things was that just once in a while, nobody really did not know whether to join the ranks of the doubter, or the worshiper of life's amazing truths.

To War, with fervour, Garbo would often go, and capture the ear of an unfortunate voyager on the good Composing ship in search of a jaunty jobbing face or extraneous sort.

It was the illest of fortunes that Garbo's work frame stood implanted alongside the cabinet containing fractions, superior and inferior figures, and all manner of meteorological signs and symbols. His knowledge on these were extensive to say the least and to say he was always ready to help with the benefit of his experience, is something of an understatement. The trouble was that with the generous assistance and help, before one could get away, came forth fast, the product of his ever-fertile mind and imagination.

Even an incident of the most minor importance was likely to provoke an episode of colour and conviction. An innocent event such as a hanging thread upon a garment, could produce the wildest of tales. The old favourite opener, comprising of both a question and an answer, would manifest itself upon a wide range of subjects and variety of occasions, to remain a firm favourite.

'See you are a coming apart at the seams, old partner.' stated the latest newcomer from the great mysterious metropolis of knowledgeable Norwich, as he attempted to make good acquaintance with all and sundry.

To actually have someone open up a conversation was truly too good an opportunity to let pass unscathed. Breathing out a cloud of light blue smoke and pursing the lips to tilt the tatty fag, heralded to those who were in the know, that a veritable snorter was in the process of being born.

The grizzly, grimy hand was raised, and two lumpy arthritic fingers curled with the thumb, to extract, and scrutinise the soggy fag end. Three long seconds of silence elapsed, then came forth with recognisable reverence, the first words of a truly remarkable account.

'May well be, master, may well be, but I'll tell you what! It's many a thread such as that which has saved a man's life.'

The innocent ear inclined with interest and obviously warranted, and yes, asked for more. There was never even an atom of doubt that he was going to receive it! None at all!

'Yes, when I was up at the front, southern Italy, as I remember, hard times boy, hard times. Many a fine man never returned home from there. Just begun getting about we had, when Jerry he start to sling every thing he had at us. Soon made us get our old heads down I can tell yeeww, master.'

'After a while, we moves up see, to this right rare farmhouse. Real splendid old place, typical of the Hun and his generosity to buildings. Like that old place up there at Ratter's Lane, expect you've a seen it, standing it out stark against the skyline on a crimson setting sun. Though you h'aint a from around these parts a here I h'understand. From Norwich, due north, aren't you?'

'Smoke and dust there was everywhere, wood and rubble, piles of bricks from shelled outhouses. Like they been strewed around by some great giant at play with his toys. A rare mess.'

'In we go, round the farmhouse, or what's left of it, to set up communications in the old buttery. Down comes another shell from Jerry, and the whole blasted ground shakes all around me. Feel it right up through my feet to the top of my head I do. Masonry and all manner of things there are heaped around us.'

The new and eager listener was much impressed and interested by this time in his blissful ignorance. 'Really,' he exclaimed. Garbo sped on eyes glinting and watery.

'Gives myself a shake I do, and brushes the dust from off my stripes. Sergeant I was see, and a man in uniform must be able to see and identify his leader, especially in times of stress. Right, I say to myself, looking round calmly, let's take a head count. Two dead, two slightly

40

injured, and one young lad just a plain shaking with shock and fear. Carnage and destruction there was in the cause of the King.'

'Hearing a low moaning and scratching sound within the rubble I see one poor beggar half covered with bricks and dust. Soon I gets all this away from him and see he is a hurt. Hurt real bad poor devil. Uniform torn apart around his stomach with a huge gash in his guts.'

'Looking closer I see most of his intestines popping out, a rare bad state. "Over here lad", I call out to the young 'un, the one who was half scared out of his young life. No use to me whatsoever is he, so I dispatch him off to the field ambulance area and radio up someone to come up and collect casualties.'

'On me own again and looking down at this poor fellow it don't take long to work out that I have got to help him somehow. Fortunately, not being afraid of blood, guts, or any damned thing of that like nature, I bend over him, then kneel down aside him.'

'Gets out the water bottle and clean my hands and the exposed parts of the wound very gently and carefully I do. Scooping his intestines in my left hand I ease them towards the wound and they start to draw back in. Soon the last bit pops in neat as you like.'

'Well, what next you might say? So did I. Then my hand wandered to my breast pocket, below my medal ribbons and I feel the military housewife. Which if you have not been a soldier, contains buttons, wool, needle and thread. Yes, friend, thread. Now you can see where I'm a coming from I expect. 'So, soon, there I am, stitch by stitch agonising the poor soul, drawing the great wound together best as I can. Just on fair finished I am when they arrive and cart the poor devil off.'

'Excitement all over I start to totter a little from my own scalp wound exposing the bone. They insist on carrying me off in spite of my protestations to continue and claims that there are plenty who are a lot worse off than me. Far more deserving cases I think and says. They was a quite right though on judging my condition, because keel over I do and pass fair out.'

'Drifting back to consciousness in the field hospital I am, laid out one of many on a row of makeshift beds, when I am aware of voices around the bed next to me.'

'You can imagine my surprise and pleasure to see the subject of my efforts with the housewife, laying smiling weekly, awaiting attention on the operating table to the foot of my own sick bed.'

'This Medical Corps captain arrived. The experienced officer leant over the man and drew back the covering from the horrendous injury. He said quite clearly, "Tell me, where is the surgeon that stitched this wound?" looking around.'

'The soldier smiled again, too weak to speak he raised his hand and motioned that it was me. With tears in his eyes the Officer turned to me, looked down at my stripes and shook me by the hand. "Thank you my man, for today you have performed far beyond the call of duty", he said.'

The saw shrieked, biting its way into the wap of picas, showering shiny shreds upon the floor. The mitre spun leaving its tiny furled rolls of soft metal beside it. The lead cutter stood as a silent sentry upon the bench awaiting its next handler to trim nonpareil or two point lead to size. Metal soldiers stood side by side ranged to read as a line of type on the galley. Modern, Old Style, Goudy Text and Plantin. The mirror image read with ease, a fact of life that right was wrong and wrong was right, in a world of black and white, with very little in between.

Thus was yet another inaugurated into the ways of Garbo's World. As he started to take the first steps away back into the land of reality he was gently, but firmly, halted. The scraggy old hand stretched out to lean across and rest on the galley racks blocking the way past.

'Where did you say you came from?' enquired Garbo. Somewhat bemused, apprehensive and more than a little perplexed, a fairly comprehensive answer was freely given, obviously hoping to terminate the conversation.

'I come from Norwich, but have been working and living in Bournemouth, and now moved back for one of the Company houses,' the young man detailed.

'Bournemouth eh, Bournemouth! Huh, I was stationed down there during the war too. Coastal defence, but a sort of recuperation to regenerate the poor old batteries so to speak,' began the ever enthusiastic Garbo.

'Top of those small cliff things. Mended the lift for 'em once I did. That's not what I remember the place for though. Best remember it I do for the events of the long wartime summer of 1943.'

'Beautiful evening it was. Yes man. Weather clean and clear, visibility good, air quality high. The sun just setting over Poole to the west and starting to throw up a lovely glow of golden hue. Poole Harbour on my right as I looked out to sea. There we are, our island, set in a silvery sea, as the poet put it. Like a mirror, hardly a ripple.'

Garbo's hand swept the imaginary horizon drawing in interest with it.

'Beautiful view that is,' interjected the unsuspecting listener, by this time determined to contribute in some manner toward the one-sided conversation.

On with even greater strength and vigour forged Garbo, barely a pause to lick the puckered lips. 'Little waves lapping the generous golden sands they were, a real treat,' he continued.

The bright eyes screwed up a little and the brow creased a fraction as the great fertility of his imaginative mind rent its full fury on the opportunity in hand.

'Yes, then all at once my attention was distracted, by what appeared to be a tiny dark pinprick on the horizon, amidst the now duck-egg blue sky. My honed senses sharpened as I percepted the first murmurings of the wailing air raid system. Siren like they blast here dinner times. Darned offensive thing! Very soon I could hear the drone of Jerry's engine as he came in low over the sea towards dear old Bournemouth.'

'Up comes me dander. Hatred and resentment rose up within me at the intrusion upon this pleasant scene. An invader to our green and pleasant land, this England, our native Country. Full of fine proud deserving people. Yes, even down there in Bournemouth!'

'Within myself I knew that a situation was about to arise from which the very best of me was to be required. The speck grew bigger and bigger as it got nearer. Stood my ground I did, damn to the warning sounds.' The eyes shone even brighter with an intensity sufficient to light a hurricane lamp. Clearly there was to be no stinting on this tale!

Garbo continued with fervour, arms bent at elbow level, chest high, swaying. 'In he came, strafing the promenade, arrogant and misguided.'

Neville made noises, and made them very well today. 'Ch-ch-ch-ch, boom, boom, da-da-da, scheeew!' he contributed adopting the pose of an evil Hun in a gun turret.

'Up comes me rifle to me shoulder. Automatically like, instilled in me from the training, now a second nature as if an extension of my arm. One up the breach instantaneously'.

The actions really did speak louder than the words!

'Could see him clear as a bell. Hun, crouched low over his controls. Mean and menacing. Threatening all good people. Taking up the first pressure on the trigger I breathed a short prayer and let go three quick shots. Rapid fire! Moving the bolt like greased lightening I was. Lee-Enfield, 303, lovely weapon that, saved many a life.'

'Jerry turned, very slightly, one wing at first, then dropped in height. Continuing the downward path his low line came to crash into the cliffs below, almost at my feet as it were. Well, I was something relieved I can tell you!'

'My thoughts were interrupted, broken the silence, by the sound of cheers. Coming down the road was a veritable throng. Singing and waving small union jacks. Seized me they did and a raised me up upon their shoulders and carried me to the town centre where I was officially thanked.'

'Always remember that I will, gratitude of the townsfolk and the Mayor. Only thing was it did not get the front page of the Bournemouth Echo. Nearly a whole page the write-up was though. Never forget that I won't, remember it for a long, long time,' said Garbo with pride in his voice.

'So will I, for a long long time, never heard anything like it,' remarked the new colleague departing in haste.

Removing the scrawny arm and inhaling the last repugnant whiff of his roll up, Garbo took his presence and stale sock smell to set a course for the far end of the room. Luba Katanga, the African bible, corrections thereof seemed remarkably uncomplicated and trivial by comparison, but almost as incomprehensible to the mere mortal souls of merry England.

OPTIMISM

Life is not what it was -

it is not what it could have been -

Life is not what it is -

But Life is what it can be!

(....but that could also be *Retirement!*)

CHAPTER FIVE

Stable Stuff

'Hello, what you got there then boy?' uttered Garbo to one of a small knot of comps gathered, before the afternoon bell sounded noisily to commence work.

'Only an odd piece of nylon fishing line, old mate,' came the reply.

Sensing that this sole and innocent information itself was enough to evoke a time-consuming saga, the gathering began immediately diminishing in size. Some were unfortunate enough to be in a position from which their route of retreat was cut off. Prisoners of the narrative to come. More fairy tales Grimm, no doubt. Very grim like as not.

So set forth our friend with liquid tongue, as silver as any gentry's spoon.

'Reminds me of the time when we used the horses hair to tie our hooks. Catch a fine roach or two on a good horse-hair hook length I could. Mind you horses! Now there is a marvellous creature, the horse. As marvellous as man himself, so I tell you, tell you I do. Takes me fair back to our poor old Rufus so it does. Right rare character he was too. A real one-off. Blind you know. Ran off one day after a swarm of bees had a stung him. Straight into a hawthorn bush he went at a terrific speed.'

'Know them great old thorns you get, well, clean poked the poor old devil's eyes out they did.' Garbo took great heart from the half-believing, half piss-taking, sympathetic *'Ah'*, *'Oh'*, and *'Really'*, interjections from the compulsive crew of the composing ship. Ignored the cynical smiles, and laced in with new vigour.

'Had a way with him when I was a lad though. Come to me where he take no notice of any other. Soon as I get me little old self along to his grazing field he'd a scent me on the slightest breeze he would.'

Everyone was quite prepared to believe this aspect of the narrative as he could be very distinctly smelled on the stillest of airs some distance away. 'Been like it since he was a child then,' Rodney muttered in a low voice.

The gruff voice grated on with the tale. 'See him raise his head and give it a great old shake as me hand open the gate. Lovely big old hoofs come pounding 'cross the meadow towards me they would.' The old eyes became glazed with a convincing truth lingering on the past.

'Always used to take a sugar knob or two in the pocket of my trousers along with me. Filched from the cupboard when mother was not a looking. Kept it in a big old stone jar with a cloth over the top. Top shelf, she did. Not a place that would deter an adventurous child though. Ay, and I was all of that you'll see.'

'Come right up to me and nuzzle in my hand, he used to. Well, a little trick or two with him I did then. One day, started to walk back to the gate and he followed me on as usual, and had me an idea. Keeping my hands

48

behind me back; in a rather cupped manner like this,' He demonstrated the position dramatically, accompanied by three short paces.

Eyebrows raised quizzically from several directions of the encaptured but not enraptured, audience. He returned to his lecturing position and posture of one outstretched arm upon the frame. The next move could not yet be anticipated.

'Blow me, darned if he don't put his big old nose into my cupped hands and just follow me along. Mind you what I have not told you is that I had kept a lump of sugar or two back, a little concealed, just to encourage him.'

'Believe me my friends, do you know after a week, poor blind old thing was a following me right into Dungate town with his nose tucked into my hands,' he triumphantly proclaimed.

'Rather a case of the blind leading the blind eh,' came Sceptic Scot's remark as he hurried gratefully away with a sardonic smile.

Garbo, not to be outdone, responded rapidly. 'More of a natural way with animals, my old Dad used to say.'

Undaunted he seized the opportunity as a drowning man a lifebelt thrown, and launched us further into his particularly peculiar world of outstanding and ever astounding credibility.

Several pairs of eyes wandered to the clock, one or two fingered the loose change in their pockets. Bodkins were examined, tweezers twirled and tweeked. One more fortunate fellow slid quietly and disloyally away. A depleted audience remained, not nearly as completely enchanted as poor blind old Rufus, but all too obviously about to be considerably enlightened yet again.

Garbo commenced with fervour, 'Going up the old Norwich Road we were, way back a fair few years ago now I am of course. Times when there were few cars and motor vehicles about these parts ripping around. Rare place in those days, East Anglia proper.'

'Peace and quiet there was, a true, and tranquil English country day. Father he say to me he do, "Boy, we'll go to Norwich market today, a see what we'll a find." Right proud I was to be going out with Dad, and a lot more than a bit excited I can tell you.'

'Got up right early we had, sun been broke through about an hour. Father, he soon had the pony and trap all kitted up. Looked a real treat it did. Straps gleaming like good leather do. Bit of sparkle on the lovely smooth hand-forged brass fittings. Craftsman made of course. Beast a standing there waiting patient and obedient. Freshly groomed by experienced hands, almost gleaming in the sun it was.'

'Sitting up beside Father in me best clothes, yes I was. Hair greased down just like his, with a bit of best butter from the cold store. Proud and pretty like a new three penny piece. Something it was then my boy, to go to market! A real day out!'

Some very heartily wished that he still went to market. Would go that day. Now in fact. Perhaps that's what made his hair stink these days, sour butter, the remnants of many years accumulations deeply engrained in the shiny scalp?

The redoubtable Robin continued, 'Got up there along by Brooke we did, when out rushes this young fellow, from a small lane on the left. Not there now of course. One of them there housing estates that spoil everything in its place. Damned shame that it is.'

'Howsomever, "Stop Master, stop, stop, please do!" he holler out, real upset we could see. Father he pull up the reins.' Garbo enacted the scene complete with a loud "hey, hey, ho," now well engrossed in the fables of his youth.

'Draw into the side we do. Young man, well, he all a twitter. "Come you now quick, Master, please do," he say, something rare distraught.'

'Off we go, with him up on the cart aside us. Following his directions we are. As we bump down the stony dirt track he tell us there been a terrible accident and his boss is hurt real bad. Father, he want to go and get the doctor straight off, but no, he's already been a sent for by the good woman of the house. Poor chap really need someone else there.'

'Parking the trap by a very large fenced paddock Father makes off with this here young fellow into the big house.'

'After several minutes, being a bit of a young Turk, I finds meself getting a bit bored, and climbs down does I. Course, next thing is a bit of a walk around. Afore long what should I see in the paddock but a horse.'

'Darned great thing it was too. Black as your hat and fine high prancing legs. Come charging over to me he do, this fine stallion, hyperactive, eyes all ablaze and looking full of fire.'

By this time Garbo's eyes also had assumed a fire of brilliance as they flashed towards the listening faces.

He looked down and gouged a considerable quantity of dirt from under the fingernails with a broken matchstick and enthusiastically continued.

'Blast, "Whoo-up, mister", I say, with confidence like, and clamber over the fence into the grassy paddock. Lovely bit of turf as I recall. Green jumped right out at you as it met the eye. Rich bit of sod. Scared, I was, a lest he do some damage hisself against the strong wood fence. Hated to see an animal hurt even in those days.'

'Still shoot the buggers now though don't you, poor old rabbits,' interjected the enterprising Essex-man.

Unmoved Garbo resumed. 'Prance right up a before of me he does, almost waving his hoofs in front of my very face. Fair feel the draught of 'em I can in the stillness of the air. Up goes me hands on to the one piece of mane I could reach as he comes down. Fast it was, like lightening. Reactions a lot faster in those young far off days they were. Not short on courage though.'

'The very instant his head start to come near me, course you know what I start to do? Blow. Yes. I blow. Blow with all the might that little old body could manage and muster. His nose comes close and I direct the breath to blow right up his nose.'

'Shake that great old fiery head he do. Side to side at first. Then a little slower up an down. My head's a going with him, blowing with him all the time.' Garbo demonstrated bobbing like an Olympic boxer in the ring.

'Starts to whinny a little then, slows down a little more. Less stomping and fracas. "Good boy", I call several times.'

'Soon calm him down that does I can assure you.' This part most of the audience accepted. The breath of the man in his maturity was reminiscent of a septic tank being emptied. Probably it had been like it since he was a child.

'I know how he must have felt,' said the very nice apprentice boy with his cultured private school voice.

Garbo drew himself up very straight and proud. 'There he is, standing, good as gold, letting me stroke that smooth strong face. Quiet as a lamb. Friends, he and I. Kindred spirits.'

'From behind me, I detect a slight movement, and a voice say, "For mercy's sake lad keep still and quiet".'

'Somewhat perplexed I turned around to see Father and the young fellow had returned. They bid me move slow and cautious away from that fine great creature and duck out under the fence.'

'Being a good lad at heart, and brought up to a do what I was told, not like some of them these days, I complied.'

'Soon as I got out, Father, he boxed me round the ears something hard. "Damned young fool," say he. Then the other fellow start to speak who had rolled up. Older man, big and strong, look like a blacksmith. "Lucky young fool, more like it", he say, and start to recount the deadly details of the day's incident.'

'There had been not one single person in that there village, whole village, mark you, that could handle this particular creature. It was a fearsome brute that had wantonly attacked three handlers outright and bitten several more. Indeed it was this very critter which had been the cause of the accident that had befell the Master of the house that very fine and sunny day.'

'In a turbulent mood the horse had several times kicked down the stable doors and careered around the place like a man possessed. Real angry. In a tempest of a storm he was. The like of which only the end had I witnessed. '

'Man speak again, he go, "Don't be too hard on the lad, Sir," to my Father quiet like. "For this young boy here have either a fine rare way with animals or an unusual talent with horses. 'Tis a gift you'll not often see. Maybe not again in your life time. I know because horses are my life."

'Father he looked something proud at me. "Up on that seat young Robin, no more antics from you today, and let's be off to Market now," he say.'

'A rattle on the bridlery, a flick of the reins, and off we go. Blast, I can tell you, I can recall the scene and sense the smells as if it were today.'

'So there you are young man, you see, horses are a little bit special too me. There is a lot that springs to the mind of a mature man from the sight of the simplest of things,' Garbo concluded as he edged away like spastic frog leaving all and sundry in a maze of modesty and mystery.

'Not in the three-thirty anywhere today is it that horse, I suppose?' asked rindy Ronnie, clutching the racing page as normal.

The incredulous and somewhat amused gathering dispersed in good humour. The work-up bell with all its noise had not moved them an inch away from hearing the end of such an epic.

The Clicker appeared from nowhere with the daily newspaper in his hand, shaking his head in disbelief. 'Look at that bugger, you would have thought that would have won at a better price than that, bloody bookmakers. What was all that about? Another one of his time-wasters I suppose?'

Boredom and misery descended once again as due depression settled itself amongst mathematical equations and extraneous sorts. . . and the world of print went on, and on . . and on . . .

CHAPTER SIX

The Seat of the Problem

It was soon after the return from a short absence for illness, that the Old Friend decided it was high time all and sundry were introduced to more of his country lore.

Naturally the disposition of his health had covered several periods of descriptive narrative. The best that could be assumed to comprise the truth, was the claim that he had indeed suffered some form of malady of the foot. For, whatever else he was, he was no malingerer. This old chap was very tough! Tough as old boots and as hard as nails.

Garbo's diagnosis had, not surprisingly, differed from that of his doctor, and further more, contained all of that very familiar quality of individual abnormality.

The crystals in the heel had been crushed making the foot hypersensitive. This was a reoccurrence of yet another old war wound, and had a tendency to leave the feeling on both feet with a truly remarkable delicacy. One foot, of course, growing in its unusual capability to match the other over a period of time, thereby producing an exact pair. This was accounted for by not some deliverance of the Lord, or faith healing, but under the general heading of the human body being a 'truly and wholly wonderful thing'.

The audience were informed that these amazing feet could, on a good day, designate and record the exact position of each nail in the shoes he was wearing on that particular occasion. Even the most minor of slight imperfection upon the concrete floor could be perceived.

Those with a less charitable and sympathetic view wished the remarkable feet had the power of mind and activity to execute their own washing, drying and powdering too.

The Letchworth Layabout proclaimed, 'Well old mate, I have heard of *feet's* of strength but never *feets* of foot!'

Something at least, was that on this occasion the Old boy had actually visited the Doctors' Surgery. Proof in itself of the visit was demonstrated by the wild waving of doctor's certificate. No one ever got the opportunity to read what was on it of course, but all were prepared to admit he was a tough old bird who did not make a fuss over much to do with ailments or injuries.

The only other instance on record to procure the attention of medical services was the awesome account of the famous 'Splinter' episode.

An unfortunate individual committed the fine folly of asking generally of the comp room if anyone was in possession of a needle. This was required for the rapid removal of a fair sized, and very deep-seated splinter in the thumb. The product of tightening the wooden quoin against a ragged side stick on the galley of type.

It may have been guessed by now that our mutual Friend was only too pleased to accept the opportunity to

56

give forth a modicum of advice. This was naturally accompanied by the normal 'better than thou' descriptive experience, conjured up in an instant.

Garbo commenced with a cheery grin. 'Down along garden, working on my dahlias I was, when up come the Misses. "What are you a doing of?", she a say to me quiet like. Then ask me if I have the time to assist her, with arranging the seating for the Ladies of the village meeting. Down at the Chapel it was. Getting out the seats and the benches. A strong reliable pair of hands required of which I fits the bill.'

'I say that I shall be right with her, puts on me coat and off we goes together on our bicycles.'

'Not afore long we arrives at the Chapel and in we go, wife having the key to open the place up. Another position of trust you see.'

'Get most of the chairs out and a few benches, with a table up the front, when my little eye, spies set at the side by the wall, a longish, about eight feet, seating bench. Standing on its own, away from the others. Lovely bit of wood.'

'Just the thing, I feel, for the very front row and an ideal place for the flowers the Wife had brought along to be displayed upon. Didn't want them on the front table in case they got knocked over.'

'Puts it into position, heavy, solid old thing, and stands back to have a look at it. My attentions are immediately drawn to the condition of the wood. Yes, looks like a bit of old deal okay. I am amazed though at the sheen and shine of it where it has become worn over the years through continual use.'

'The regular presence of the human body clad in coarse materials had taken its toll. How many bums has sat themselves, young and old, over the years I cannot tell you. What was sure, is the effect they had together created. A polish as fine, and smooth, as any man could ever make by design.'

'I lets me hand run along the line of the fine grain. Confirms my earlier opinion of it being a fine piece of deal. Towards the centre I notice the odd spot of roughness under my finger tips but nothing can be seen by the eye. Not even my beady pair.'

'Amazing,' contributed the setter from Solent showing genuine interest.

Garbo resumed, oblivious of the comment. 'Down on the bench I sit myself. Place my hands either side of me on the bench. All of a sudden it comes upon me to slide myself from side to side on the bench where I sit. Slow at first, and only an inch or two, then a bit quicker and longer like.'

'How very erotic', interjected the large bearded Australian listener with his usual accent.

Garbo continued unmoved. 'The Wife she a holler out we are ready to go. Job done.'

'Can't resist one fast final move. Quite sharp like. Instantly I experience a sharp surprise though. Excruciating pain enters my lower body. Fair enough to make an intake of breath. I then realise what has happened. It's that damned tiny rough piece I had detected.'

'A great old splinter had raised itself and run itself rare straight through the coarse weave of my trousers right into my blasted behind. Nipped clean through one cheek and into the other. Pinned together the flesh as neat as you like. Fair near made me a holler out I can tell you. Very nasty!'

'Very', was the general contribution from several bystanders listening intently.

'Sat there I am damned near petrified to move. Wife she keep a hollering us being a' ready to go. Damned annoying I find it in my moment of pain I can tell you.'

Some laughed outright, their eyes watering, others smiled in mirth. No one was taking up the option to leave this time.

Garbo continued. 'Summoning up all the courage a man can muster when in need, I force myself upwards and away from the offensive wood I had now come to heartily dislike.'

The Mancurian Marxist interrupted, he couldn't resist it. 'What you call *tearing the arse out of it*, I suppose,' he said smirking.

Garbo found no cause for cryptic comment on the remark, scowled, and continued fluently.

'Wife arrive in a huff. Most unsympathetic. Call me an old fool for not asking why that one bench was set away from the others and only seldom now used. Similar slight experiences had been suffered before but nothing a like this, I can tell you. That's damned gratitude I thinks to myself and have to hobble off nearly two miles to the doctor's house. Can't get back on the old trusty steed of a cycle by reason of my physical condition, so to speak.'

'When doctor cut away the cloth of my trousers he can hardly believe his eyes at the size of the foreign body.'

'Got a great big old donger, then have you? A heavy old hampton, so to speak eh, big Bluey?', crudely commented the antagonistic Australian, feeling this indeed was his day.

Many could not believe their ears, when amidst Garbo's adventures such irreverence was executed. This interjection verged on the outrageous, but enhanced and even made more enjoyable, this entertaining tale.

'Gives me a local anaesthetic, he does, out with the scalpel and makes a few incisions in the delicate area. On to the damned tweezers. Removes the offensive article and nips a dose of disinfectant on with a couple of plasters. Makes me wince it do, and blinking old eyes water a bit.'

'What you call getting to the *seat* of the problem I suppose,' said the West-country wonder boy.

'Tells me he do, that in forty years of practice he never seen nothing like it, bar when in India strange sights he'd a seen,' the narrator stated ignoring the interjection.

Garbo bent leant back over the immaculate frame to continue working, terminating the tale with his final comment. 'But to answer your question. No, I ain't got no needle!'

Some fine far off day, it was mutually decided, the Composing Chapel Committee room could travel to India, perchance therein, to conduct a survey. To observe and establish whether bottom splinters, are, of common fact and good in size, within that particular quarter of the globe.

The whole saga left the original incident of the splinter in a very meagre light. It encouraged many to express to the poor unfortunate fellow who instigated the epic, that he, really was, making a considerable fuss over bugger all in comparison.

Much impressed he grumpily departed, holding the injured finger which had endured much prodding from various helpful people during the telling of the tale, to no good effect. No doubt the good Company nurse would administer the usual iodine after her needle work and provide a finger stall, and *that,* would be likely to induce a further episode.

Garbo was indeed great with his imagination and memory. An entertainer of considerable quality, who broke up many dull and dreary days with a smile.

Even the extensively detailed narrative of a hair which had decided to grow the wrong way, turning in, as opposed to out, did not measure up to this sorry saga of the 'seat' splinter.

That particularly unusual and highly offensive follicle, on the 'chinny-chin-chin', as he called it, had an historical flavour. The site of the scourge having been created by a very bad nick from a two-hundred year old cut throat razor, which, believe it or not, had been in possession of the family for generations.

It was reputed to have belonged in the past, to a long lost sea-going, pirate relative. A bastard uncle, related, distantly, to the Prince of Wales, on his mother's side, and hence the throne of England. A true and heraldic connection to Royal patronage, no less!

Having grown warily away from the wound, the versatile hair, had appeared on the inside of the mouth. In the first instance as a growth, the size of a match head, including the root. Whereupon it was painlessly removed and discarded to places unknown having first been offered to medical science, but rejected for its use.

Yes, things were always complicated in Garbo's world, and he was certainly a King of something. . .

DEPRESSION

The darkest day before the dawn,
seems rich in bitter bloom,
as fosters there a fallen hope,
as withered prize kept bloom.
Industrious effort may lay wrecked,
thoughts clear rent asunder,
from hope, despair, in agony claps,
as loud as clouds in thunder.
Beware the thought that keeps you down,
to grovel at your knees,
whilst others triumph in your loss, and whine,
'why, yes sir! Please!
It's me, not him; it's him not me,
the best, the worst, the liar.'
Shake off the foot upon your neck,
that keeps you in the mire,
stand up, strike out, look on,
speak forth, an individual you,
fear not the way to stand alone,
for what you feel is true.
The time shall come for all to see,
what common man holds dear,
his dignity, his person - as
himself from year to year!
Trouble not on conflict views,
that please the mewling kind,
more give yourself the room to find,
an equal feeling mind!

CHAPTER SEVEN

A Tall Story?

To return to the matter of the Countryside, series and insane scenes, well, they were delivered with the normal vehemence and eccentricity at the most inopportune of moments. Occasionally Garbo would excel himself and not interrupt production, as seemed his dedicated crusade in life.

'Just walked across the Marshes,' he started up, as three or four were gathered to devour either their sandwiches or the rolls from the Company trolley.

The selected potential audience were seated on the upturned metal waste bins and there was no escape. The aroma of the Great unwashed and the blue smoke from his roll-up did nothing to add to the flavour of the victuals or the atmosphere to eat in.

Invariably, if the ash did not drop upon the tatty waistcoat or filthy apron, it would find its way into someone's tea. At least this was better than the repulsive snuff that continually blemished his handkerchiefs or accumulated into a brown drip on the end of his nose.

Garbo continued his quest upon this chosen day and munching motley crew.

'And arrived down by the river, when old dog she started to get excited. Run about with her tail in the air to say she was on to something.'

'Couldn't see a darn thing except an old willow. When I say old I mean one of those with a good girth on too. As big round as three men stood together strong and true. One of those snobbed ones. You knows what I mean. Every year or two they cuts the top out of it, leaving the foliage short. Pollarded, we say.'

'Anyway there she is hard up against the river; always like to call a willow a lady mind you. Think of an oak as a man though I do for some reason. Howsomever, the trunk it is angled away from the bank. Leaning out over the river. Damn near forty five degrees I expect, which is unusual for a tree of that shape. Pushed that a way by the constant pressure of the prevailing wind I wonders, during the period of its growth on the exposed spot.'

'Expect you seen the sort of thing occasionally by the road side, but not angled to the same degree yourself, eh, I'll warrant?'

The lunch time sustenance continued to disappear into hungry mouths. One rude rival immersed himself into the racing page of the Daily Mirror, and another gazed longingly at the great naked breasts displayed on page three of a surly Sun gutter press edition. No one risked interruption.

'Get right up to the willow I do and see the dog, she's real excited about something alright. All of a sudden out of the corner of my beady little old eye I discern the faintest of movements. Same trained eye that has spotted many a Jerry sniper in its day I can tell you. Slight movement then signalled life and death in those dark days.'

'Didn't have the opportunity to see close movement often then. Would be anything up to half a mile away. Maybe just a dot on the landscape. Officer's, they used to pick a good country lad with a keen eye and sense for detail. Man who could absorb and become absorbed into the terrain of the country. Pleased to say I was such a man in my prime. Anyway that's another story for another day.'

The silent unspoken reaction was undoubtedly along the lines of gratitude. War and Peace by Tolstoy was short in comparison to Garbo's assorted adventures!

Garbo had twisted his neck to thrust the bald head into an aware listening position. Frozen in action. A master of the stage as well as the story! Normal posture was temporarily resumed. Then, soonly supplemented by a further repeat demonstration, he continued with marked enthusiasm.

'No more than a flicker it is. Round comes me head in an instant. Senses honed you see. At first, not a thing can I see. Mind you I have pinned the movement to a small specific area. Plotted and contained within the mind in an instant!'

'Put myself right hard close against the trunk of the tree. Place my ear very steadily and silently against the bark of the tree. Listen hard I do. Within that gnarled old willow I can percept the faintest of vibrations. Blast boy, something is right down inside there somewhere. Raise the interest immediately it do. Now what is that likely to be I wonder? The mind conjuring up several pictures in a trice'.

'Stretching up I grasp the top of the rough bark and gradually ease myself up. Just as I get to eye level with the pruned top. . . Whoop! Something shoot out over the top of my ole head fast, drop towards the grass. Drop the head down does I, fast as lightening.'

'Dog she shoot off like a rocket. Make a fair speed she do across a marsh with a bit of open ground on it. Trained you see. Open air animal as well as domesticated. Nose down, head up. She'll be back with something. That I blooming well know!'

'Unperturbed I find a fractional toe hold and have one hand holding on, and the other now free to feel into the crown of the tree. Bit of a hollow like. The Queen she is about to yield up one of her little secrets sitting there aside the river I know to myself.'

'Blast, Hello, I can feel something darned furry in there. Blast again, yes! Yes indeed! A bit of movement. Up we goes a little further till I can see much better amidst the growth, into the well of the tree.'

'God, bless my soul. There we are, can hardly believe it myself. Snuggled up close together now, what do you a think I darned saw?'

'The mind absolutely boggles,' the Concrete Kid from lousy London offered.

Then after a second or two of silence he tried again.

'Wasn't a couple of cats was it?' he guessed half-heartedly with a wry grin on his face.

Garbo gazed down in utter disgust. He conjectured that these Townies probably only ever saw a cat or dog as the animal alternative to human life in their confined world of the terraced house and in-city urban jungle.

He still managed to respond with out prejudice and with some kindness in his voice.

'No, my young friend it was not cats. Not even a wild one, and I've seen one or two of them in my time. There, seven foot up a tree, hanging out over a river, the like of which I guarantee you will never have a seen in all your life!' Garbo paused and shifted position to maximise the suspense and wonderment of the tale.

'Was a nest of baby rabbits. One two three four. Five, he demonstrated the counting process with a bobbing of his head with furrowed brow.

'Six, seven, eight. Nine did I say? No, I lie. Ten! Blinking ten of the little blighters! Not a week old I shouldn't think. Surprise for me I can tell you.'

After a few seconds pause Garbo queried, 'What do you think of that then?'

'Not bad, Not bad at all,' answered the Townie. 'Most people have only seen rabbits produced from a top hat. "*Unbelievable*", I think is the word I'm looking for!'

'Nasty little bastards the old coneys are cobber. Shit and make bloody holes all over the place at home. Mind you they not so stupid over there as to try and live up trees,' the Australian contributed.

'Thought it was all upside down and they would fall out of a tree anyway down under,' said some wally.

'You never want to be surprised at the Lord's creatures anywhere. He moves in many mysterious ways his wonders to perform,' the Lay Preacher quoted.

'Well, he certainly constructed a weird and wonderful sodding mystery when he made Old Robin here. He's full of surprises,' a visiting stereotyper laughed.

Off went Garbo to fiddle about on his frame much gratified by the tribute to his originality.

The surprise element of his tales had generally long ceased to exist and impress the normal audience. It had regrettably worn off for most of the listeners many pence ago. It was in fact, only the variations of the presentations which held the daily intrigue. The

67

expressive gesticulations and grimaces, or the caustic comments from the comrades under the inflicted inferences of their ignorance.

The swing of a sidestick, the sweep of an arm. Fingers which poked, pointed, and made paper quiver. The menace, the scowl, the hatred and the frown. None more generous than when directed towards the hated Hun.

The tanned teeth, and the nostrils endowed with a fresh brown crust of snuff, that would be of sufficient quality, and ready, to challenge the reputation of Hovis. This was the only human that emerged from such an individual mould of the Lord God of all creation.

Were the unwilling witnesses of wanton words and wisdom grateful?

Well, some days anyway, in amongst the six point sorts. and machine revises with breaking back bent across the bed.

After all as many said. 'He ain't a bad old boy. Bloody good craftsman! Just a bit different, that's all!'

The Power and the Glory

The prospective employee stood at the frame with the Union's Clearance Card in his hand waiting for the FOC to appear.

Interviewing with the Company was nearly complete, the promises made were now to be discussed with the famously elected representative, and our prime print worker had an opportunity to 'meet the men'.

'Actually, you know, I came here myself by the very special invitation,' Yorkie offered in an opening of probing contentious conversation.

'Yup, me too! I came from the other side of the world in answer to an advertisement for my rare skills,' added Aussie.

One of the immigrant City Slickers joined in. 'Loads of promises, promises, but not a bad place. Only trouble is we a'int had a decent night's sleep since we've been here. Birds singing, cockerels crowing, then the peace and quiet frightens you mate! It's bloody diabolical.'

'Well, none of you blighters were wanted here really. All totally unnecessary! I hate the blasted lot of you,' the

Lay Preacher commented demonstrating his sour but sincere Christian feelings.

Garbo's turn. 'None of you *foreigners* were bred half properly anyway,' he quipped looking for an entry.

'Where is the FOC anyway?' asked the Overseer, keen to avert yet another inter-galactic wrangle on the best of breeding.

'Down the bog. Gone for a Gutenburg,' piped up the Scouser selecting sorts for his press revised edition.

The respected Father arrived, wiping his hands on his apron. It was rumoured Dangal never washed them if he was about to shake hands with the Management.

'Who we got here today then, mate? Another Lord Lucan or someone else calling themselves John Bonfield? We had Enid Blyton's husband here last week claiming his expenses for the day,' he said grinning broadly and offering his hand.

He took the green card and examined the details. 'Yes. NGA okay. None of these damned demarcating SLADE interlopers,' he announced to several present from the dreaded Committee.

Normally a positive answer to the next question guaranteed automatic entry to the Companionship.

'Involved with the Chapel where you work are you, Old son?' the FOC asked innocuously.

He had hand-picked his Chapel Officials from all over the Country from those who had applied, to build up the war machine that was his weapon - *The Composing Chapel Committee!*

'Yes, Comrade. Party member no less. Clerk of the Chapel. On the Fair List. Ready to black any bastard! Here's me card, paid up full, no arrears!' was the ready response.

'Nuff said. All done. Give the man the job!' proclaimed the Father fiercely to nods and mutterings of approval all round.

The composing room manager departed looking extremely disappointed, but there were few about with skills for the intricate chemical formulae workings that were required. The Oracle had spoken and the new man would start with rest of the rabble rousers.

At least the day had started well for Dangal the FOC.

Ten o'clock arrived. Cheese rolls purchased from the canteen trolley were ready to be eagerly consumed. The 'dis' tins were in position with empty galleys across the tops for makeshift seats.

Mugs and cups of tea and coffee were on half pulled out cases and the floor. The *Daily Mirror* and its fellow tabloids were being unfolded for reading, and the world was at peace - well, as usual -almost.

Ausie arrived on the scene, in a hurry, to disturb and dismay the assembled throng.

'Move please, Parson, I want the 14pt Goudy Text Caps case out,' he antagonistically addressed the Lay Preacher, now comfortably entrenched in front of the frame feeding.

'Always got to be a blasted nuisance have you not, damned menace!' moaned the miserable moving man.

The lanky long fellow lent over the case he had drawn out and expostulated wind, loud, long and clear from his backside.

'Ahhhhh! Meet the good Abbott and four pints of his Ale,' he exclaimed in gleeful relief at the proud passing.

The aroma hung heavy, humid and reprehensibly revolting, Most decided there seemed little option but to escape from it - a hurried mass evacuation.

'Oah! Oooh! Disgusting when people are eating,' gasped the choking Lay Preacher furiously, his face puffy and red in anger.

'Terrible! Bastard ought to be Chapelled for that,' Percy moaned as his tea was slopped over his apron in the hurried exodus.

'Right, I will! Father! Mr FOC! I have a motion,' called the Lay Preacher stiflingly from under his nose-covering handkerchief.

'Have you a seconder? If so, let's bloody hear it then,' said the long-suffering FOC in his dulcet south London tones., almost tasting the smell himself.

Percy's stubby pencil scrawled upon the galley slip as the Plaintiff announced his words.

"This Chapel deplores the ungentlemanly conduct of this our evil Australian brother and demands severe punishment be imposed!"

'I'll second that,' said the petulant Percy.

The intrepid FOC scrutinized the piece of paper and took in the comment from the Australian that, 'Bollocks! Even evil gentlemen fart!'

He crossed out the offending words and substituted *anti-social and unhygenic.* This was good fortune indeed. He had been waiting for an opportunity to lightly disrupt production and punish the Management since another fruitless complaint about the leaking roof had failed to get a good result.

The well-worn silver whistle came out the apron pocket and was blown thrice with considerable force.

Amidst cheers and dutiful bidding work stopped. A mechanical silence prevailed as comps and casters crept from corners and keyboard operators stumbled gleefully down the stairs escaping their penance at the boards.

Amidst much frivolity, jest and seriousness, the motion was read by the Clerk of the Chapel to the assembly of canny craftsmen.

More happy humour and humiliation followed as the perpetration of the sin upon the aggrieved members of the Chapel was explained. Questions were asked about one certain pair of underpants and looseness of the bowels, then paper, pegs and pints.

'Are there any amendments then ?' called the Father eventually.

'Yes, remove last four words, and substitute *"imposes a fine of ten shillings"!'* called the waistcoated stonehand standing with two fingers in the chest pocket. His moustache bristled with his importance and pride as he adjusted the angle of his glasses.

Seconding was done by the grey-coated gentleman from the proofing press. He hauled out his watch on the silver chain from his pocket, checked the time and snapped the face lid shut with a resounding click, then raised his hand aloft.

'We must have rules and respect, Comrades. I so do second for a solace bought out of time,' he said.

'Right. All in favour, now please show,' called the FOC. The show of raised voting hands was unanimous amidst cat calls, whistles, words, and ideas of farting for Australia.

The Father commenced his words of wisdom for the minutes, posterity, and long custom of the true trade.

'Brothers, we are joined together in this dreadful place, from all corners of the globe. The spirit of our Companionship must prevail with good will amongst each other. In the same way we have come together over this awful instance, we must strive together against the iniquities and injustices of the Barbarians, our employers, and the abominable bonus scheme they inflict upon us.'

'Mr Chairman, talking of Barbarians can I say,' began Garbo.

'Meeting closed' snapped the FOC. The Company had been disciplined by the disruption sufficiently in his opinion and he was well aware of how long a tale from Garbo could take. The last thing he wanted now was to lose control of the situation.

He smiled in anticipation of the outrage upstairs in the Boardroom where the issue would be adjudged an outlandish waste of time and money.

The Managing Director's hand shook with rage as he sipped from the gold-lipped china tea cup. 'Revengeful bastard! Was complaining about a hole in the roof last week no body has been able to find.'

Mr Chairman shifted his considerable bulk in the padded arm chair and blew a stream of smoke upwards from his Senior Service tipped cigarette, unmoved as usual. Paused, and responded.

'Ungrateful sods, the lot of them. Thought they would have been glad of the extra bit of fresh air on this occasion!' Bloody Townies!'

CHAPTER SEVEN - AGAIN!
(*Must be a Printer's Error!*)

Antics and Adversity

The new first-year apprentice had just returned from his search for a circular 'chase', and Garbo's crabby mouth beamed from ear to ear. There was a great love of all things traditional in the Industry for him. The age-old japes were ageless, and the humiliation of youth a great pleasure in its innocence for the passing of yet another day of boredom.

When ever an apprenticeship was fully completed and some one *'came out of their time'*, a good old traditional banging-out took place in the Comp room at Dungate just the same as every other printing office, large or small. Nobody beat more vigorously upon the galley and frame than Garbo. It was part of his world that remained unchanged, unlike the seasons of the year which passed by with their own crop of hardy annual tales tailored for each and every occasion.

The swallows on the wire waiting to migrate usually instigated some wild autumnal dream or drama of far off places. It was not only Arthur Ransome who had Swallows and Amazons in inventive form, some of

Garbo's truly amazonian tales took a great deal of swallowing.

No one really knew for sure that he had not been here, there, or everywhere, in his war-time wanderings. It was like everything else, there was just that glint of possibility and credibility hanging tantalisingly, partially invisible, like a gossamer thread from a complicated woven web waiting to trap the unwary victim.

The motley crew of the Composing ship always expected the Oak and the Ash - the soak and the dash to come out in spring. The red sky at night with the shepherd's diabolical delight and dreaded 'morning' warning.

Our human barometer wielding type scale and composing stick, could forecast the weather better than the television or radio and was remarkably reliable.

The brown dried seaweed adorned his frame to be crunched between the eager fingers for a forecast. The prophet of doom would make his serious pronouncement of imminent storms and much turbulence. Then busily batten down the hatches and strategically place rusty cans around the room with a determined importance to catch drips from the still leaking roof.

Was confirmation devastatingly assured because of the feeling in his bones and a conglomeration of other fanciful philosophies? Never! Not a chance! It was all down to *'experience'*, or so he said!

On the frostiest of days, heaped upon the greatly adored marshes there was always an abundance of mole hills to be seen. Standing out sharply against the soft green grass the brown bumps were usually capped with a light white dusting of frost in winter-time. Earth heaps frozen as hard as the rest of the ground around and sometimes the wily water's edges as the Waveney wandered its way down slowly to the sea.

A cold, clear, sharp day, with a touch of sun, or maybe one of where rafts of sunlight are breaking through Prussian blue skies making seagulls stand out startlingly white, as they soar on a breeze. It was all Garbo's terrain and undisputed domain.

The molehills were not all the same to Garbo. Oh no, not to the sharp-eyed Norfolk Nightmare as he pushed the pedals round on the trusty steed. Any slight change had been observed and transmitted through the eagle eyes to the amazing memory of the merchandiser.

'Did you see the signs of rain today, boys?' enquired Garbo of those within earshot.

'No, not read the paper, or had the telly on before I came to work,' replied the Cockney, sincerely offering what he considered to be the best information, in a helpful way.

'Rubbish! Man's modern methods not required! Mother nature talks to us!' Garbo stated with great positive confidence and authority.

'How do you make that out today Robin? Cold is set in for sure now I would have thought?' enquired Yorkie.

'That's where you're all a wrong again Master, see. You are in the lowlands now. None of yer towering hills and craggy rocks around here to depress everyone,' the Ultimate Authority proclaimed.

'See, old Mr Mole, he a knows in his skin and his feet when a change is going to take place. Remarkable little beast that he is! So do the earthworm. Barometric pressure changes he senses too if you like as well. Soon as he know that, those little old paws throw up the earth as he head upstairs for the open air.'

'Mark my words, and mark them well, there will be rain afore you go home at dinner time, or on your way there.' The crafty face was wreathed in smiles.

No one argued, they knew better than that. True to form as the hands of the clocked clicked to high noon, the patter of raindrops could be heard on the angled glass roof overhead.

'What did I tell you! Raining!' hooted the triumphant Garbo.

'So is the bleeding Queen, but she don't keep on about,' said the irritable Cockney at the thought of yet another long interruption.

'Right, you are reliable Robin,' soothed Gorgeous Georgeous nicely, and the old chap's face showed his pleasure and broken teeth.

'Mother Nature she wins again, and we'll all be the wetter for it into the bargain,' was Garbo's parting shot as he headed for the loo.

Neville smirked and made his own prediction.

'He's off for a crap now. Always does when it rains so he doesn't have to get wet walking down the garden path to the outside privvy at home in his lunch hour.'

It was thoroughly outrageous for Yorkie to poke in his own allegedly Northern home grown sayings, in his confident and convincing manner, whenever things went a little quiet.

He eyed Garbo's after dinner arrival, in the dripping cycle cape, showering droplets everywhere and upon all and sundry. Congestion and confusion fought with each other for space.

Yorkie announced broadly, *'If doocks be on t' water in November, t'will be rain in December!'* Or so they say up home!'

78

'Load of hogwash', retorted Garbo unconvinced with a snarl. This was clearly a challenge to his rightful position of overlord of all happenings and phenomena natural. In addition he did not like arriving at work wet and to the accompaniment of much extraction of the proverbial urine.

It was the Londoner's turn to spin the wheel a little next. A friendly pointed prod to help things along like.

'Down our way they say if the mice come up from down in the cellars it's going to rain,' he contributed seriously.

'What push up the paving slabs do they?' asked the Lincolnshire Lad, labelled the 'Long-haired Lout' by Garbo on a particularly bad day. The nick-name had stuck and the curly shoulder length-hair had stayed in defiance.

'Well, they all talk blooming rubbish from down there anyway, Goldilocks,' said Garbo a little heatedly.

'Good on you Cobber and right you are. What do the mice do next? Stand on the roof with their umbrellas up wearing wellingtons, eh, Smokey Joe?' the Australian mocked.

'Well what's so fucking unusual mate, about your dry, godforsaken, bleeding wasteland of a hell-hole home then, arsehole?' the Cockney retorted raucously.

'Kangaroos, bluey. Kangaroos. Know what they say do you? *If a kangy he hop, then it's real sure to say,'* he paused noting the interest and let the conclusion hang on the air, drawing everybody on.

'Come on then, finish the bloody thing, you are getting as bad as Robin,' said Merseyman with interest.

'He'll shit on the path as well as the hay, you pommy bastards!' roared Aussie with laughter, mirthful tears

coming to his eyes as most of the congregation moaned and jeered aloud in their humour together.

'Always has to have filth in it doesn't it, you blinking heathen,' the Lay Preacher muttered.

Garbo snatched the opportunity like the best of all great performers and stage troopers, deciding the past properties of rain were now exhausted for the moment.

'There is plenty that is good about a drop of manure. It reminds me of the time. . .' he said twirling the first available sidestick as a bandmaster's mace.

'When we was in North Africa chasing Rommel and hunting the Hun. Ah, now there is a place with another strange collection of god's cratters if ever I saw one.'

'Been in the desert for about two months. Sun fierce every day, dry out your mouth and nose. Eyes a burning themselves into their sockets with the same heat as the very sun itself. Blasted terrible hole for a mortal to be cast into for sure. Don't seem to affect the animal and insect inhabitants though, suppose they've 'hadjisted' themselves used to it under mother nature's apron, century upon century. Thousands and thousands of years to develop amongst the millions of grains and their natural environment.'

Garbo's flow was temporarily stemmed by the cool Concrete Kid, seemingly obviously prepared to draw on experience once again from the deprived depths of the Metropolis, tactlessly set against the background of his new area of domicile.

'Rather like the local people from round here do, eh? Stand around gawping in their bleedin' cornfields all day,' he jibed.

A few sniggers crept out accompanied by hoots of derision, whistles and cock crowing's from the floor.

80

Garbo physically winced at the slight upon his genetic connections and proceeded with much malice well concealed, but growing in his heart.

'Once wondered to myself, on a fine bright night, whether there was more grains of sand in the Sahara desert than there were stars in the galaxy.'

'Worried my mind as I turned it over for days. Constellations and consternation's so to speak. Never did decide though. Any way that's not what I was about to say. Beside the point.'

The grubby strong fingers turned the edges of the sheaf of copy laid on the galley barrow and picked them up to knock them into a sharp neat pile. Garbo stroked them very precisely and replaced them on the barrow with a long heavy piece of six em lead furniture on top to hold them down.

His head raised and the glimmer of anticipated revenge shone with a brilliance from his eyes.

'See, there is very little moisture in a place like that, not even at night. Amazing how the life exists in such strange surroundings. Adapt you see, they can. We are the interlopers, we are the strangers, we are the ones with the funny ways intruding upon these quiet quaint crattrurs in their peculiar private place.'

Aussie saw the opportunity to prod the Londoner with a side stick. 'Just like these Cockneys coming round here Robin. Bloody invaders, sticking out like a sore thumb. Unnatural sort of beasts!'

The Concrete Kid said nothing and thrust his hands deep into the apron to retrieve a half a bar of chocolate from amongst odd sorts and bits of lead, to feast upon.

'Indeed, you may be right,' Garbo grinned and continued.

'Well this bright burning day we was a sat in the shade of the canvas slung overhead with nothing much to do, when an almighty ant come crawling along. The desert's strongest creature for its size and a predominant pest at times.'

'Little old legs a going, carrying a bit of paper he'd a found in front of him, to take for a nest somewhere I'll be bound'

'Now this blighter was all of an inch long if it was a whisker wide. Fat, man, well you have never seen anything like it. Fair bloated with its shiny brown body bulging. Biggest damned ant any of us had ever seen.'

There was a pause as the Old man assessed the impact to date, and he transfixed the resented rival from the inner city wastelands with his beady eyes.

'Crossed my mind to train it and tame it, make a pet of it. But no, no, no fine sirs! Wrong for a wild thing to be retained in such a wide open space methinks. Like being shut up in this blasted place! Whilst we watch, that blinking old ant, it stop short and start to darn well relieve itself.'

'Raise a fair hoot it does among my military comrades of the time, fine fellows that they are. Soon commands a crowd around when there is little else to do.'

The well-appointed format of pause, pose and pounce was developing for our master narrator.

'Old ant he just a keep on crapping. Bless my soul. . .'

The Australian intervened, 'And my hole.'

Garbo glowered and resumed the tale ignoring the contribution.

'You would not have believed the size of the turd that came from that little body. It was as long as itself and damned near just as wide. That tiny body strained and every muscle, twitched every hairy bristle, every leg and antenna vibrated.'

Garbo paused, ready to savour his moment of premeditated triumph as his hand stretched to lay itself kindly upon the shoulder of the Concrete Kid.

'In fact, my young friend, it was just like some people I know of, not too far away! Absolutely so full of shite you would not believe it!'

Hoots of laughter rollicked around the room, and a grinning Garbo went off to his frame.

The Concrete Kid spoke with some trace of offence and small hurt in his voice.

'I am only surprised, my old son, that you are not claiming it had the ingenuity to wipe its arse on a piece of paper as well,' he said as he stuffed the final pieces of the chocolate in his mouth.

'Now that would be wholly unjust,' replied Garbo over his shoulder.

'It's only the human that has adapted himself to such a filthy habit!'

Satisfied he had made the last word in conclusion the narrator took position at his frame. He spat forcibly upon the floor and scrutinized the proof before him.

The precarious production of print went on.

Heads bowed low and shoulders stooped over the frames. Bodkins poked and tweezers pried their way between the shiny spaces of the metal letters.

Over the far side of the room the monotype casters crashed and clicked away as the door opened to let out their noise. Inside the mechanical monsters menacingly spewed forth their issue.

Characters and spaces from the molten metal. Lines and leads for quads and queries.

Words emerged from casters and turned themselves into sentences. Each one as variable in content as the distance of a star. Silver amongst the blackness of the coming ink. Twinkling and travelling outwards through learning and light years.

A mumbo jumbo of the coded cataclysm which so compounded the compositor's wealth in the strange ways of words and workings in their Industrially incestuous world.

Every galley would become divided into calculated pages, emerging eventually to influence the mind and eye of an ardent reader for tomorrow. Shaping the future and recording the wonders of the past.

CHAPTER EIGHT

Of Mice and Men

It was unfortunate everyone had to work. Lucky it was that all were able to go home at the end of it each day. Amongst the bold and the brave who ventured home daily for dinner was Garbo. Undaunted by the two miles each way he totally refused to have anything to do with the Work's canteen.

Garbo's journeys back and forth were a constant source of remarkable happenings as one might expect. The 'voyage incredible' was loaded to the brim with events. . .unusual!

Nothing was more likely to prompt further narrative than a work mate's related experience after dinner. If you had nearly knocked a cat over, well he would do better. One had its head lodged in his front wheel, and thrown him off into gigantic nettles.

You had seen a bad accident? Well then, he had seen something twice as darned disastrous.

That had to be anticipated as normal procedure. Not often did he dwell on the macabre, but when he did they were gems. Often his trusted steed of a cycle, well oiled, paint gleaming, would feature foremost.

'Just got down there toward the Dam on my bike I had, and was distracted. Hey up, by a strange sound from the wheel in front.'

'What in hell's name is that, I thinks to meself? Look down in to the darkness towards the front wheel. Eyes attempting to pierce the ray of light from the headlight, on to the tyre beneath. Powerful dynamo it is, throws the light way, way, in front of me. Few nice little modifications I've made myself powered it up a bit you see, boy.'

'Well, blasted thing is shining well away from the tyre and I knows if I stops it will be straight into the gloom of the night with nothing to see by. Dynamo driver on the wheel need movement as well you know.'

'Soon the next street light comes into view as I complete my passage over the unlit section. I look hard and try to see what is making the noise. It is all too obvious to me that some alien object has adhered itself to the tyre.'

'As the wheel rotates on the smoothly oiled bearings it is catching on the mudguard. Making a little tick of a sound with regularity, slowing as I do.'

'Apply the brakes, and cruise to a smooth stop, and dismounts I do. Hard as I might look, I has a right darn difficult job to see anything at first.'

Actions speak louder than words. They were executed with professional panache, bobbing, bending, in a mock inspection comparable to a fine Sir Lawrence Olivier performance.

'Then, there, in the glow of the street light I sees it. A small oval object catches my eye. Very, very slowly the wheel is turned back. On closer examination there is a shock for me, I can hardly believe my eyes! Stuck very firmly to the tyre, in the centre of the tread is a nail. I know what you're a going to say now,' said Garbo.

Several listeners jumped for the opportunity of audience participation and choroused, 'What's so unusual about that?'

'Ah Ha!' said the ever enterprising Garbo with great glee, enthused by the piss-taking participation.

'It was not an h'ordinary nail!'

As if everyone present hadn't guessed.

'No master. This was no h'ordinary nail as the likes of you boys has seen afore!'

There was a poignant pause to heighten the anticipation and a fearsome glower was swept along the adorative audience challenging disbelief.

'It was a human nail. A finger nail! Right so, it was. Small, and clearly been pulled out by the root. Still with a bit of gool and a tiny fragment of flesh attached to it. Fair made me look I can tell you.'

'Reckon it came from a young woman's hand, 'cos there, in the half light, with an eye that's been a trained to adjust to the dimness of lights.'

He was rudely interrupted by bearded Barry. 'Only one eye, what was a matter with the other one?'

'I shall ignore that stupid remark, everyone knows what I means 'cept you,' said Garbo coldly.

He continued now determined even more to impress the adoring audience.

'I could just discern the faintest traces of nail varnish. Not easy amongst the colour of the blood, but, I did. Was going to keep it, but no, I flicks it with my finger. Won't move, can't budge it. The sharp edge of it set it slightly into the rubber. Get's out the trusty old blade from my pocket and opens it up. Fine Sheffield steel, rare nice antelope horn handle, hand made of course. Soon prize the little devil away that does.'

'Blast, I think, as I rides home, this will be the rarest cause of a puncture you have ever had if the tyre goes down. Didn't though. Dunlop never lets you down!'

Surveying and absorbing the silence he concluded aptly, 'Now what do you think of that then?'

'I thought it was Durex, that never let you down,' said Paddy bearing in mind the Pope's purity and power

'That's why he's got eight kids,' said Titty amidst making up pages, to everyone's amusement.

'Not a very nice bedtime story at all,' said Thomo the ten-point terror resuming work with a smile.

Nobody wanted to think on about Garbo's stories. No one was that keen to lose their sanity.

Our Robin 'Garbo' Gray, had other ideas though. Unparalleled in originality and encompassing all of the normal incredible dramatic role plays, his very best actions were some of those entitled by his dutiful sufferers, as 'The Chapel in the Valley' series.

'Coming out of the Chapel we were, on Sunday morning,' the nauseous Norfolk narrator began.

'No doubt praying for forgiveness about all the lies he tells,' muttered Meryll.

'When the old Vicar he say to me, "Ah, Mr Gray, my good friend, my blessing to you and your good lady wife. I understand you are something of an expert on the ways of wild creatures. I believe you can help the Lord and I in his house here".'

The bright eyes twinkled challenging disbelief.

'Bit a taken aback when he go on to say that local opinion has it that I may be the only man about who can help him. Took me by surprise, but as the wife often do say, I'm sort of famous in the village for the things that a happen to me.'

He paused to extract the grubby handkerchief from his pocket, wave it and then snort loudly, horrible snuffy things into it.

'Don't know why I'm sure, but, there you are,' he said.

'Famous here too, mate,' said one of the Londoners with great feeling.

'Anyway, I asks him what his trouble is, and it's not long afore he is a telling me of the problem. The mice have become an awful curse upon the place. Causing a rare bit of bother here and there they are.'

'What with distracting old ladies during prayers and looking as though they are going to run up their legs to you know where. Making young women call, out in horror. Then of course, you got the young varmits from the school enjoying it all and giggling in the prayers.'

'Coming after the Communion bread they are, and things arriving at a pretty pass with attendance's falling.'

'Smiling to myself I can see the complications of setting mousetraps in such a place. This I knew called for something different. An entirely new approach. Cunning required.'

To acknowledge the search for the Holy Grail is one thing. To acknowledge a pursuit of the holy mice is another. Indeed it would now so appear that within those humble walls, the Good Lord was about to "move in many mysterious ways, his wonders to perform".

The challenge of working directly for God was guaranteed to bring forth the very best in our Friend. All things, it is said, are possible through prayer. The things that were possible through the grace of Garbo were truly to be acknowledged as miracles in their own right!

Garbo continued to take them down the tale track, or was it the garden path, with enthusiasm and zeal?

'So, home we goes, and I applies me mind to the situation in hand. It's not long before I realise that I shall have to return to the, scene of the crime, so to speak.'

'First of all I want to establish their most active period. Even their feeding pattern. All live creatures must eat. Man, he identify that aspect as the hunter, and he is in advantage. Creature not always so wary when an eating. Besides that, funny things are mice. Crafty.'

'Get along to the Chapel straight away like, I do. Has entry with the Wife's cleaner's key, and takes a good look round I do.'

Garbo weaved and bobbed, shaded his eyes. Moved his head up, down, sideways. Here was the hunter at his very best. All the instincts of man honed to a fine precision for pursuit.

'Eventually, with all the nooks and crannies of the fine old building examined, I come to a definite decision as to where the little blighters are holding out.'

'Deducing from the faint trace of dust disturbed, along the edge of one of the stained glass window sills, I knows there is activity in the area. My eye had then travelled over the window itself, in all its beauty. Each piece settled neatly in its hand made leaden encasement. Craftsman been at work again, plain to see.'

'There, not easy to see amongst the many colours as the sun shone through, was a small hole. Using my natural instincts I know that, and it becomes very plain, they are making their way, through the hole, and then along the top of the highly polished pew. Blast, I can also detect the minute scratches of their tiny paws on the varnish. Get along to the end of the pew they do, drop down to the umbrella stand, then down to the floor with a quick scamper I'll be bound.'

'Jump a lot do mice. Like cats you know. Not got a fear of being airborne. Funny creatures. Least to those who do not understand them they are, that is. Eh, Townie?' he concluded temporarily.

'We have fucking great rats, in towns, Mate. Big as bleeding buses. Not puny little mices! Beat that bugger!' he said with considerable feeling.

Garbo continued unimpressed. 'Returning home I knows just what I have to do. Gather a few articles together.'

'Bit of wire, string, bottle, then into the kitchen. No cheese though. Oh, no. I don't take no cheese. Surprise you does it, that? No, cheese too obvious. Calls for subtlety this job. Requires something original, no mess either. No poison in the house of the Lord.'

'Fits up all me contraption, pliers in the pocket, last look round, and off we goes again. Back down the Chapel.'

'Just makes a quick call in at the Vicar's place to tell him everything is under control. A plan is devised. Invite him to the Chapel at seven the next morning. Meet him afore work in this damn place.'

'Bit a time at the Chapel, fiddling here and there, and it's off home. All we can do now is wait and see. I've done my devilish worst. Not that I think that sounds quite right for the Chapel,' he sniggered gleefully.

The Lay Preacher felt it opportune and his position to interject at any mention of the Church, or for that matter the *Chapel* if it related to the Union organisation.

'Well we have the very devil in the Chapel here, causing trouble and unrest. Upsetting everyone. Failing

91

to honour the ways of the Lord or established practice,' he whined.

'Shut up and get on with your bloody work, windbag,' the Father of the Chapel retorted invoking more muttering from our troubled friend of the great and mighty king of all compositors in the heaven above.

Not bothered in the least bit Garbo continued.

'Next morning, lovely clear crisp sunny day. After I have put the old cut throat razor across the stubble on me face, it's breakfast.'

'Wife been outside a poking about in the hen house. Productive task none the less!'

'Nice fresh egg the brown hen has laid for me. You know one of those real big 'uns, two yokes. Know how to spot them I do, so do my little old Gal. Blast yes, just at a glance the way they lay is good enough. Gets that into me with a fresh baked crust from the bread and off I goes to the Chapel.'

'Edge the door open quiet like, stealthy and silent, makes me way down to the one pew I'm interested in. Straight away I can see I have been successful.'

'Now, what I did not tell you, was how the trap had been made,' the voice cackled and crackled with the zenith of the episode clearly about to be revealed.

'Fixed up on the pew I had a very large jam jar. Sort of suspended like with the wire I mentioned earlier. So, you see, when mouse, he come along the pew, get he to the end and a jump. Down he plop, into the bottle.'

'Now then, he might jump out, or scrab his way up the edge of the glass sides and away. How did we get over that?'

'We'll, I shall tell you, friends. Filled the jar to within two inches of the top with salad cream!'

'Other mice they come along, attracted by the smell and the activity. Carefully tread on it and in they goes too. There you are. When I looks into the bottle there is nine of the little varmits, dead as a door nail.'

'Why? 'Cause you know,' Garbo paused and heightened the anticipation of an answer to the amazing scheme.

'Mice can't swim in salad cream!' he said grinning.

'Vicar he arrive and is something blinking surprised and appreciative I can tell you!'

The listeners were speechless.

He turned towards the nearby proofing press. Took a palette knife and dug it carefully into the tin of pliable ink and smeared some on the roller.

After replacing the lid firmly with a tap, the ink roller was brandished in the hand, shiny and black on its surface. Deftly it was applied to the surface of the ink slab, suck, slick, suck, slick it echoed as it rolled adhesively across the plate.

The aroma of fresh ink filled the air and paper was duly applied. . . it was the only proof Garbo ever had!

THE COMPOSITOR'S COLIC

It isn't the way that I work that I hate,
deep down I don't care if I'm early or late,
it's hardly the bore of the black and the white,
and who gives two damns if I'm wrong or I'm right.

The absence of windows, the gleam of the sun,
one hardly has noticed, when day has been done.
The patience and fiddling's a perpetual trial,
the dirt and the ink, from my home just one mile.

It stands out offensive, on the Common a blot,
to the Waveney beauty, one sore septic spot.
But is it the factory, and work my old mate,
or is it in fact - just yourself that you hate?

CHAPTER NINE

A Bit of a Plant

Some very wise poetic fellow in time fair past spoke forth to say, *'O to see ourselves as others see us'*. It was something of an enigma to know how Garbo even wanted others to see him. Perhaps he was too busy engrossed in dreaming up the next instalment to bother himself. What a great variety he had to offer!

Old Ernie was not too well at home recovering from the removal of his haemorrhoids, and the Father of the Chapel was to visit. He had purchased a potted plant from the Market Place during the dinner hour and it resided upon the top of the frame.

Garbo duly informed one and all of the Latin name and fingered the shiny green leaves delicately. Never one to miss an opportunity to impress his followers further, he commenced his next narrative with an innocent sounding statement.

'Funny you should have bought one of those you know. Haven't seen any about for a few years now. Used to be very common at Christmas time a few seasons ago, and reasonably priced too.'

'I have grown them from seed myself mind you. Can't remember whether it was Japan or Australia I sent off to for the stock. Took a fair time to arrive. Do quite remember they were uncommonly hard to get hold of though, believe I saw them advertised in a catalogue. One of those there specialist publications that are difficult to come by.'

'Mind you it is not much that I ever buy in the way of seeds. Like a little cutting I do. Don't have to be much. Bit of healthy stem, preferably with a bit of heel on it.'

'You know, one of the best places I've a had some of my best cuttings from is Sandringham. Day out on the coach with the Wife and me nail scissors and we always come back loaded. Full of all sorts of goodies for the greenhouse is her handbag.'

'Got plants that have been sprung from shoots in Kew Gardens, almost tropical some of them.'

'Then all those bits and pieces we've got from Sandringham are a little bit special see. There is a good reason for that. Yes, master. A damn good reason.'

Garbo waited. Surely someone would be inquisitive enough to ask. It only needed a slight clearing of the throat from an innocent bystander to provide the incentive.

'Yes. Not long been off the coach and walking round the grounds. Lovely gardens there. When I was aware that we had become isolated and apart from the rest of the coach party. Almost sort of ostracised, like.'

'Feet again,' muttered the foundry Clicker quietly.

Beside us stood a very well dressed woman, in a most expensive looking blue pastel shaded suit and a large brimmed hat. It was the clothes that impressed me first. Standing proud and dignified, with bonny bearing she

96

was. Then it was the voice. Had a sort of familiar ring to it. Cultured like.'

'With a sort of regality it said, "I believe I know that face, from times of war," with an air about it.'

'I looked up and felt something proud. Wife she looked all a twitter.'

'I bowed slightly and said, "Yes, Ma'am, your guard of honour at the Palace when the bombs fell. Got to know each other pretty well then I think." War time see, not all bad.'

'Well, the Queen Mother, God bless Her, she asks me what we was a doing there on the day. Bit of a stupid question really, but I told Her of our h'interest in plants.'

'Dare not tell Her I had come to nick cuttings. With a twinkle in her eye she say to me, she does, "Mr Gray," she say, "If you would like to take cuttings from our greenhouse do be my guest. You have my personal permission and I shall mention your name to my head keeper over there".'

Garbo delivered the quotation with a slightly affected accent and then continued normally.

'Blast, I was something appreciative. Set me up for years it has you know! To get back to where I was now. The plant.'

Those smooth little round marble-like berries are the main feature, green at first, then turning to a yellow through to a cheery bright red. Anyway, as I was a telling you of, had not seen any about for a few years.'

'That was of course until I was on my way a back to work just now. Bottom of Bridge Street hill I am. Just got off me bike, getting a bit ancient to ride up there now. When down the hill towards me come a great fat old brute of a woman on her bicycle.'

'Big old machine too, one of those sit up and beg types with the curved frame. Coming quite fast she is, in a straight old line, propelled by the gravity of her own weight.'

'Hey up! Trouble afoot, or aboard I should say. All of a sudden she hit a rut in the road. Bump, bump she goes as both wheels pass in and out of it. Wonder how she stay seated on the saddle.'

'A very faint dash of colour passing to the ground catches my attention. Blood is that I thinks to myself, no it can't be?'

'Much to my amazement, that tiny speck of colour is getting a little bit bigger as it comes towards me, down the steep hill.'

'It gets nearer and nearer, and I stoop a little to improve the line of vision.'

Garbo crouched lower shading the allegedly straining eyes with his hand, and continued. 'Nearer and nearer. Bigger and bigger. Closer and closer. Sure enough it finishes its rolling journey down the hill to stop at my very feet.'

'It has my deepest sympathy,' said the Letchworth Layabout rubbing his nose.

Garbo, totally oblivious to any personal relevance, straightened up and continued.

'Puzzled at first I hold it in my fingers, roll its smoothness around between my finger and thumb, and then raise it up towards the sun for a better light. I say to the little red ball that he's no stranger after all. Yes, you've got it. He's from off of one of them there plants.'

'Old gal, she must have had one of those plants you got standing there, in the cycle basket, on the front of her old bike. She'd a been to market no doubt too.'

'Course the jolt of the rut had shaken one of those berries straight off. Now wasn't that something of a coincidence?' Garbo finished with a twist of his nose and an application of snuff.

'Sounds jolly much like a load of *balls*, to me,' said tall Terry moving away.

'A coincidence indeed,' remarked the forever co-operative George the second. He was looking like a Pakistani after an overdose of home grown sun under the UV light. It was the first time in days anyone had spoken to him in English, and he was prepared to find any way back to popularity away from jest and well intended ridicule.

'Remarkable, and almost unbelievable,' emphasised the important Branch President setting a line.

Garbo's gnarled fingers very purposefully layered the cord around the page, firmly tying it, he poked the end in with the ancient bodkin, and slid the page up to the head of the galley. Contentedly he sighed and rolled himself yet another slim tobacco wonder to choke on.

The passing Managing Director noticed at least half of the room were working and was grateful that yet another iniquitous Chapel meeting was not taking place. He knew the branch lay official was for ever looking for opportunities to justify his existence and hoped he was not down to drum up business with his stirring spoon in the pot.

Silence descended, and the bonus scheme minutes went on the timesheets in true testimony of what had not been done this day, but would be paid for by a little perjurious pencil work.

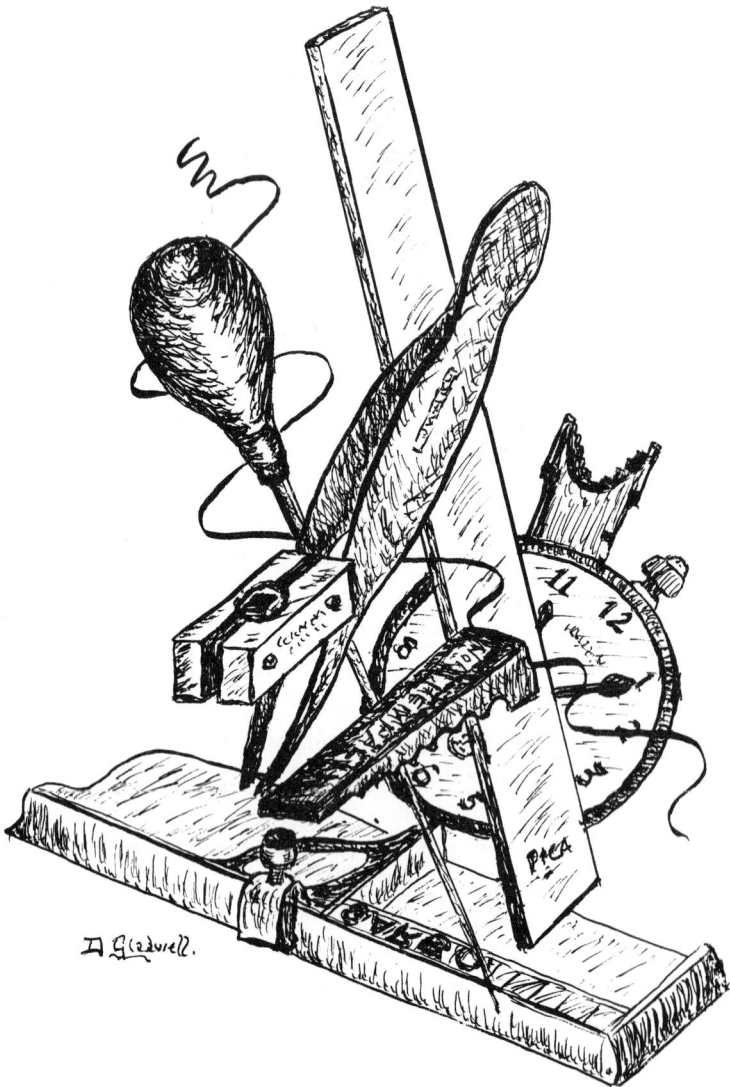

D. Gladwell.

CHAPTER TEN

Flights of Fancy

Many were surprised that our Friend never acquired a sore throat or tongue with the amount of talking he conducted. The long-suffering and experienced Percy attuned the very well- rehearsed deaf ear and sunk his head low over the frame, determinedly in the non-listening mode.

Disaster, Oh, disaster. Garbo moved purposefully westwards towards wayward workers. Resolutely in search of a listener. Merciless in his cause.

'Riding along I was you know, on my way to work this morning, and I'll warrant you'll never guess what sprung to mind.'

Alas, thought the potential victims, no doubt you are about to tell us all. Noting the unitedly maintained and disappointed silence he continued.

'Saw a grand flight of ducks going across them marshes on the Dam. Blast, fair remind me it did, of the time when I was on me way home one evening from a not particularly remarkable day of very trying tabular work here.'

From the adjacent frame the unsympathetic Andrew, well within earshot, launched into three loudly presented choruses of, *"Here we go, here we go, here we go,"* in unmelodious tone. Garbo continued undeterred.

'Looked up, did I, and saw a fine flock of birds a coming in, lovely formation, right down over the Church spire. Grand sight in the approaching evening. On the still of the air I could even hear their wings a whistling and whispering from that height. Mind you I have got a keen sense of hearing.'

'Bang, bang goes a gun well off to me right. Down comes one bird with a crash into the gorse. The other one peck in flight then drop he down towards the road, not great shots but respectable performance like, just not clean.'

'Get I along the road a little further, and what do I see? You've guessed it, there walking down the centre of the road is the other duck. Right I say to myself, catch that my man and you and the old Gal have yourself a dinner.'

'Off the old bike I gets and takes the jacket off me back right smartly and start to creep up behind him. Knew it was him, same one, because my eye had absorbed all its individual marking in the instant he started to fall. Marked so well he was, fine bird.'

'Just as I'm about to pounce I hear the noise of an approaching vehicle, damn and blast! Great old car arrives with a distinguished looking gentleman in it. "Hold you hard master", I say to him, "while I catch this here little old blighter".'

'Crouch low I do, set fairly forward on the toes. Coat stretched out before me, a shielding my presence so to speak. Quiet, relaxed, confident. Ready for a swift

102

movement in my old age. Can still do it though! Don't take me very long I can tell you...got the varmit! Lovely word that varmit!'

Nobody dared tell him it was var *mint!*

'Mind you I was a bit unsure 'bout the chap so I didn't do its neck in front of him with my fine fingers. This chap say to me that it's the most extraordinary thing he has seen in a long time. Huh! I think to myself, you should have been with me a week or two back on the marshes with my gun.'

'Yes', the tardy Tablet-taker responded somewhat weakly, anticipating that this was going to be one of Garbo's famous duo, two instalments in one efforts. The cash register could veritably be heard ringing up the precious lost pence per minute.

Undeterred continued he, as a valiant in the dark of night, eyes shining as bright as new coins, face warped with a craggy lined smile. Breath tainted, feet largely aromatic. Cheese and garlic in one! All were to suffer, that was a certainty

'Down be I by the Maltings there, walking towards young Terry's marshes, you know him, there that married the girl James, whose father used to keep pigs up by the Hall road. Nice bit of land, good bit of pasture, fine vision.'

Those from *'away'*, knew nothing of this particular heraldry or genetic syndrome but remained silent, hoping, in vain, to reduce the bonus time lost, and endeavouring to manoeuvre themselves into a working position of effectiveness.

The Company Owner scowled across in passing by.

'Dog by my side she was, fine gal, gun strain, lovely coat. You know who her father was?'

'I remember, I remember', some hastily cried, to ward off further detail. Or worse, a dreaded contribution of a tale within a tale suffered and despised by many.

'Ah, yes, well, no sooner had I got within range of the big dyke there, than up got a great old cock pheasant, all his colours shown to me, feathers pressed close to his body by the speed of his flight.'

'Up come the gun to my shoulder. Twelve bore, hammer gun, beautiful ribbed Damascus barrels, lovely engraving on the metal work.'

How well all knew that wretched firing piece, and many of its truly descriptive and amazing epics. It must have been worth its weight in gold from time lost alone!

Out came the snuff box, the pinch was positively placed and disappeared without trace to fire the caverns of the mind via the bristling nostrils.

'Just about to pull the finely balanced trigger, when there out of the corner of my eye, way up as high as any church tower, come a lone duck I see. Draw straight on to it I do, sure, steady, lead a bit and let him have the choke barrel, Down he start to come, dead in the air.'

'Well, do you know, much to my surprise it goes and catches this old cock bird full square on the back and brings him down too. Bet he was something surprised.'

Garbo glanced round to take stock of how the tale was being received. The Concrete Kid sneezed.

As the dialogue was now moved beyond the 'incredible', the attentions were waning and several heads bowed with busy fingers tickling the type.

Something to reinstitute the attention was obviously now required. The sharp eyes searched for a saviour.

He closed his hand round the wooden mallet on the galley barrow, and lowered it to his side.

104

'Blast me, the thump on the ground of the pair of them, put an old hare up, right at my feet.'

With an ear splitting clang the mallet head met the side of the half full used type throw-away tin.

Poor Hurrican Hill nearly jumped out of his skin and pied three lines.

'Prat! Stupid prat!' he shouted in true terrible torment.

Garbo grinned and continued.

'Must have nearly been standing on him. Course I soon swung round on him then and darned soon gave him the second barrel. Imperial choke for the distance shot. Lovely old hammer gun. Old dog was a bit confused to know which way to go first.'

'Soon put her right with a point of the hand. More meat on a hare and a rare good meal the way my old Gal cook it. There now, what do you blooming think of that?' said our Garbo beaming.

Avoiding the temptation to say it was all rubbish the excuses were made to hastily get on, escape at last.

Puttering Pete, now clearly recovered from his minor disaster, came in somewhat strongly with a short melodious rendition of, *"We'll meet again, don't know where, don't know when. . ."*

Four steps away the great Garbo turned on his heel with his conclusion.

'Tell me a story, tell me a story, tell me a story before I go to bed!' sang the wretched long-haired lad who played the guitar and was nearing the end of his apprenticeship.

Garbo appeared to dutifully oblige.

'Oh, yes, I didn't tell you, did I. That there duck I caught with the coat. Put him on my handlebars and he stayed there perched 'til I got home. Tame and obedient as hell. Kept it we now have, fattening him up we are, lovely meal he'll make I know'.

It was a full moon, and nobody wanted to be told anymore stories and kept their heads well down. They were all full and complete to the brim. Virtually choking with it!

Hastening their castings out of earshot the linotypes clinked and whirred, busily redistributing their brass matrixes with noise to their long metal-slotted homes, as the lengthy iron arms dropped towards the pots of molten metal.

Hard words, real words and letters, fused into a single slug. Together making a story themselves to be told and sold on the byways and highways of the outside world of wonderland.

The galley slaves worked on, and on, and on, fingers selecting slugs, dividing into proper pages with pre-set headlines and folios. Romance for Mills and Boon enthusiasts in a dream world of their own - far more boring and removed from reality than Garbo's epics.

CHAPTER ELEVEN

The Mug Shot

'Nothing is more pleasing than to see a nice bit of wood that has been turned by the skill of the fingers, and appreciation of the eye, into something lasting and attractive,' proclaimed Garbo in a knowledgeable way that appeared very final.

It was however very soon qualified away from any such connotation.

'Mind you, it's how one treats the piece of wood, the very first time it enters your hands that counts. Most important that, don't ever forget it.' He looked round the few victims he had managed to isolate for the gospel according to Garbo of the day.

'Taken all that time to grow and should be treated with respect. Like tools. Now my tools are not just a few bits and pieces gathered together in a shop and purchased. They are a fine body of instruments selected from all parts of the globe. This great and wonderful world of ours we live in. Craftsmen of all colours.'

Darkie Downton shifted his chocolate coloured body about with embarrassment hoping this was not a tale of ethnic origin constructed purely for his benefit. He could get very nasty over Garbo's 'nig nog' narratives as he would very soon find out if he was not careful!

'Jerry, he make a damn fine tool you know, always have. Take my electric drill for instance, ordinary shop purchased model. No darned use going in for anything else than the basic and then paying twice as much as you want to.'

'Make all the modifications meself I do to my tools and equipment. You can if you've got your head screwed on right. 'Scuse the pun, I suppose I should say!' Garbo said with a broad grin displaying the brown bottom set of teeth.

'Look at that lovely electric drill of mine. Unique it is! Some of the pieces I required for my modifications could not even be obtained in this Country. Had to be made to my own specifications especially, in Sweden. Blast if they didn't mill the pieces for nothing in the end, so impressed with the plans of my modifications they were,' he emphasised with pride in his voice.

'Has a very unusual *twist* to it that does,' said Lennie the lively linotype operator who had come to lean, learn, and listen.

Garbo carried on in the same old way eager to impress a new potential prey.

'Always using the initiative in the old brain box, you see,' he said tapping the temple of the bald head.

'Take my chisels again. First job I does with a chisel I have come by, is to throw the handle away and then turn up me own on the old lathe. Turn it from the very best bit of old ancient oak. I keeps it by for the job. Years old it is. Turn and trim that little old piece of wood until that fit my hand like it's known me for years.'

'Heard a tale or two, those tools, over the years I'll be bound,' said Neville knowingly.

'Nothing quite like a good *screw*,' said Aussie, seeing the opportunity to introduce the crudeness he knew irritated poor old Garbo so.

Garbo continued and the gleam entering his eye was the forewarning of an expansion of the theme on wood or tools. Which would it be?

'Like I was saying, wood, though a common everyday material, should be treated with respect. Each piece is a bit of history itself. A sort of minor monument to time.'

'One piece stand out in my mind more than any other. A very clear recollection,' he shifted into a more permanent and relaxed position. No eager crouch in anticipation of enacted heroism or despair this time.

'Got along to Lowestoft, on the bus we had. Bought some fair old pieces of crude untrimmed wood off the harbour wall. Merchants getting rid of what had come out of the sea. Had 'em under me arm in a bundle tied up with an old bit of string. Always keeps a little in my pocket in case of emergencies. Some others there selling bits that had come out of an old boat. Mahogany, Hemlock. All sorts of polished pieces to be had. Few of them goes in the Wife's canvas carrier bag.'

'Just as we are a leaving, a chappie standing with his saw in his hand ask me if I would like a real rare old bit of wood. You know me, got a nose for the unusual,' said an increasingly enthusiastic Garbo.

'And an unusual nose,' contributed the Concrete Kid.

'Right, Master, you are!' Garbo smiled and continued. 'Beside him is a real old bit of wood. Unhewn with the bark all round three sides of it. Bit been stripped of the front and sawn flat. Blast, I would really like that, but it's too big for me to manage on the bus back home. I tell him the problem and he say not to worry, he's a coming over our way in the week, five bob for the wood, and a half a crown for delivery, and it will be on my doorstep.'

'Damn me, I not got enough money on me for that. Son, he dig deep in his pocket and buy me the bugger for my birthday. He's a something tickled buying me a bit of tree for five bob. Tells me it looks green around the edges it do, and a hope I'm not. Blasted cheek.'

'I say to him to wait till in the week when it is in my workshop and I set about it. We might be in for a surprise.' Garbo's eyes narrowed as they swept the listeners' faces.

'See I'd noticed something odd about that piece of gnarled trunk. Had a peculiar swelling and distortion to the bark. A disturbance erupting from the inside.'

'Once before I had bought an old piece of wood like that. Not as big mark you. Cutting it open I finds there, stuck inside the grain of the wood, an old .45 western bullet head. Entombed in the American deal since who knows when and what over!'

'Now in me head this swelling had rung that particular alarm bell to fire the memory,' Garbo gleamed.

'And fire the imagination too, I should think,' said Southampton's very own Silly Sam!

'Come the middle of the week, the boy has come round to view the surgical operation. Quite excited at the prospect he is too. He knows his old Dad is never too far wrong.'

'Cut her down to size bit by bit, together on the two handed saw. Stacking the bits by the window on racks so they won't warp. Comes to the last bit! The special bit. The bit with the lump. Needs a special bit of treatment this one. Take it right careful we do. Still as thick round as a man's waist it is.'

'Best mallet and a favourite old heavy chisel of mine that's seen me through many a fine job, and off we goes. Few gentle chippings away at the bark around the edge.'

'Come twenty minutes, man, we've shifted plenty of it away gently. Chisel halt a little. Cutting edge clearly impeded. Look at the steel, and it is slightly impaired. Nothing much to worry about. Soon get that honed back on the oilstone. Look at the wood and what do I see?'

The look upon Garbo's face contained feigned surprise. He shifted his body in pretence of peering down at the wood.

'Blast I can see a sliver of shining silver. Get's us right excited it do I can tell you. Making a few strategic saw cuts we split the wood away slowly in sections.'

Some of the listeners wished he would get on with the job so they could get on with theirs.

'Very soon we can see the shape of things to come. Then triumphantly we remove the last bit.'

Garbo paused to remove the dribble of spit from his wet lower lip with the back of his wrinkled hand, suspending the essence of the tale to the last minute. Brothers Grimm would have been proud of him!

'Some time, years and years ago, see, some old farmer, or one of his labourers, must have sat down to drink his beer in the open air, and rested his mug in the fork or in a niche in the young tree. Walked off never to return, probably by some ill fortune or other.'

'Quite forgotten over the years it had somehow become grown into the trunk of the tree, causing the

111

distortion I had noted. There before our eyes, was that very pewter mug!'

'Fair near in mint condition too. Still got it on my shelf at home I have. Polished it up, bit of buffing and a soft cloth, revealed the date. 1622!' Garbo glowered round challenging disbelief.

'What do you think of that then?' he queried.

'Can *beerly* believe it', a weak voice croaked from the rapidly departing wee fat figure of the Lay Preacher. Long oversize apron, once white, and now grubby, trailing below his knees almost to the floor. The bald head glistened five feet one above the black shiny shoes. The podgy neck, stretching the shirt collar and tie. The grumpy grunter represented all that was unattractive about Christianity to his colleagues.

The cleaner arrived. Our Ernie, with new technology in the shape of the very large vacuum cleaner at his side. With an awkwardness that must have taken hours of rehearsal, he commenced to knock over everything in sight. The effort culminated in jarring Garbo's frame and knocking over the six point sorts he was about to lift as a line into a wide chemical table.

'Pyed it now, look at you,' Garbo angrily ranted. 'Overpaid, under worked, typically useless bloody Arab.' It was a rare show of temper, and caused smiles all round.

The Clerk of the Chapel stretched and yawned. He decided he now had enough of scientific journals for one day and thought it time to cause trouble to break the boredom.

'Let's have a Chapel meeting,' he called out hopefully.

'Go and collect some arrears, for half an hour. I'm a bit busy now,' said the FOC.

CHAPTER TWELVE

May-bee?

The time had clearly come around again for one of the dreaded and time consuming trips over the marshes, hand in hand with our constructive and creative Friend.

Recently there had been a weather balloon with recording instruments found on the beloved boggy marshes which was subsequently reported in the local press. Garbo felt it very deeply that he had not been the one to find the contraption. It became very apparent that those unfortunates of the Chapel in the vicinity were all to pay for the lack of the discovery in the very near future. Some epic adventure of astonishing proportions would no doubt be related in an attempt to re-establish the prowess of the natural king of the wet lands.

The composing ship were not to be disappointed. Oh, no. Not even just one tiny little bit!

'Going across the marshes with the little old dog, I was, when the ear detect a faint noise way off. Something approaching in the sky. Straining my eyes and senses to their very limit I perceive a small speck in the distance.'

'By the very nature of its peculiar movement in the sky, it was immediately recognisable as a helicopter. Must say I did not take very much notice of it at first though.'

'All too soon it was very obvious to me that there was something unusual, even very menacing in the angle of approach of this latter day abortion of a contraption.'

'Blast me, the blessed craft's noise got louder and became absolutely terrific as it got nearer and nearer.'

'Before long I could feel the wind from the propellers, well blades I think you calls them, moving the few hairs I have got on me head.'

'Quite a hair-raising event then,' contributed the ever alert Southend setting saint .

Garbo ignored the interruption. 'Dog she makes off as fast as whatever she can. Quick as her legs will carry her over to the other side of the marsh.'

'Next, what do I know, but the infernal machine is bearing down on top of me. Forcing me to my knees, hovering threateningly above me. Deafened by the noise, no one can hear my shouts. Stuck under the craft my movements are not noticed either.'

'In a flash I rolls on stomach, in an effort to get away. All my old army training comes back in an instant. Arms outstretched, I flatten myself, forcing my body as far into the ground as I can. Still it descends, down and down, nearer, to become totally overbearing to me!'

'The pollen and dust is drawn up from the grass and ground by the whirling blades, forced into my mouth and nostrils! Too parched with dirt, dust and dread, I lay helpless in fear and submission beneath the monster!'

'What like a virgin about to be raped?' questioned the obnoxious little Lay Preacher.

'More like an ant under foot,' said Garbo wildly, and then continued eyes ablaze.

'Just as the wheels are about to touch my back, she hold a little, and raise a foot or so with a bit of a lurch.'

'Summoning all my strength I roll over and over, fast, seeking and finding a small depression in the ground out of the way of the beast.'

'All of a sudden a young fellow jumps out of the helicopter and snatches something from off of the ground, quick like. He leaps back quicker than greased lightening into the diabolical machine of the air, and before you can say "Jack Robinson", she lurches up and away in no time at all. Like a vanishing trick almost.'

'Gone as quickly as it had arrived, it has put the breeze up me fairly. Get's me wind back and locates the dog. Takes me a fair time to get her back under control and all. Been frightened see, had her confidence shattered.'

'Then I starts thinking about the event. It suddenly dawns on me that my subconscious mind has retained a picture of the snatched up article, so it has.'

'Now I can't be sure of this of course, but I reckons it was another of those meteorological measuring instrument machine things again. Suppose they had tracked it down with an internal radio sonar device of some description. I had just happened to be unfortunate enough to be in the exact spot.'

'Only thing that puzzle me is that the dog didn't find it. Pretty sharp she is,' Garbo said pausing.

'And you, old mate, were feeling pretty *flat*, I believe you said, eh,' said a proof reader waiting on a query.

'Ah, yes, but not as flat as I have been though.'

Oh, no, it was an opening for a dreaded double dose!

'There's now't that has ever put me so flat on me back as when I was stung by two hundred and forty-one bees. Always remember that I will,' Garbo commenced.

The already disbelieving Lay Preacher was trapped into remaining and expressing his very lightly alleged interest. He looked somewhat uncomfortable as several people poked his ample fat bum with their galley sidesticks from behind him.

'Just got home and finished my tea, when who should arrive on the doorstep but the village bobby. Fair out of breath he was from running down the street.'

Yorkie interjected, 'Not come for his bowler hat back, I hope!' he said recalling an earlier tale.

'Not so,' said Garbo. 'He ask me to come along as fast as ever I can. "Mr Gray, Sir", he say, "If ever there was a man needed at this moment of crisis it is you." Tell me the three o'clock train has been held up at the level crossing gate for near an hour. Be disaster if it is not cleared afore the next 'un come along.'

'Terrible performance, yes, there had a been. On approaching the bend before the gate the Loco driver had received the emergency signal to stop. He had geared the great old gal to a grinding halt with all anchors on.'

'Toot! Toot! Chchchochoo!' shouted the Skipton Son!

'Getting out of his cab and a running down the line, he find a motor car with the occupants in a rare state of panic.'

'With the windows open on account of it being a fine day, and going slow to cross the line at the appointed place as it were, a bee had entered the vehicle and tried to settle on the driver. Caused a bit of a fuss and a stir. You know what it's like. He had stopped and in a trice,

116

afore they knew where they a were, the darned car was a full of bees a buzzing everywhere.'

'Course, bit of panic and movement and the honey bee lash out. Wild creature after all. Old bees they start to sting. Poor devil's in terrible pain.'

'Having great presence of mind, a man similar to myself, the Engine driver, he get the passengers out as fast as he can and slam the doors shut. Not I might add without getting a few stings hisself.'

'Next thing of course, they go haring off to find the local bobby. Up to the village police house to inform him of the catastrophe and seek assistance.'

'Yes, you got it right again, Neville, can see you nodding your wise little old head!'

'That's where I come into the game. Straight away he thinks of me, and the way I have with these creatures.'

'See a few year ago, I did keep a bee or two, and provide honey and the royal jelly for several of the sick in the village. Nothing big like, only in a small way. Well known for it like though, throughout all of Norfolk. Even up there at Sandringham, by you know who.'

'N-n-not the old B-b-biddy with the p-p-pastel suit again, you d-d-don't mean,' stammered out the man from the Midlands in an unpatriotic tone.

Undeterred as usual, Garbo continued to extol the great virtues of his ways.

'Up I gets and puts me boots on. Goes to the shed. Out we comes with a big cardboard box. Sort all the corn flake packets come in. Off we goes to the scene of the excitement!'

'Blast, there is a crowd gathered there okay. News travels fast I am on the way obviously.'

117

Several felt it appropriate at this juncture to reverently chorus, 'obviously!' with smiles and a faint cheer from the remote Merseyside mocker.

'Copper he is full of it. "Make way, Make way. Let Mr Gray through now please", I hears him say.'

'Soon as they recognise me the crowd part. I can sense and discern the expectation on the air. There are faint murmurings and whispers running through the crowd. It is only a second or two before it breaks into a small round of applause for me. Gives me a bit of confidence it do!'

'Peering into the car I can see the little varmits are buzzing everywhere. Great old swarm of them. Some still fair enraged with the situation it is clear. I know exactly what is to be done.'

'Putting the bee net well over me face and neck, I boldly opens the car door and quickly moves to get inside. The hum seem loud enough to deafen me.'

'Then I start to feel a bee or two searching me out. The stings start in unprotected areas, hardly notice them at first. Round the ankles like.'

'I knows that to shift these bees, and do what is expected of me, I must find the Queen. It's not easy. Then I notice there is a concentration and collection, no gathering I should say, in one place. Looks promising. Yes, it's her!'

'Stings appear to be coming on every part of my body as the blasted cratters have found their way inside my trousers and cuffs. I'm as enraged as they are now, in my frantic efforts to capture the Queen.'

'Keeping my head, I gently pluck her majesty from the throne she has chosen, and gestilate, gesticlate, or whatever, to the Officer to open the car door. Although getting on in years he leap to comply with my instructions like a new policeman fresh out of college.'

'Thrusting myself out and over towards the box in one movement, I place the Queen at the bottom. Weak by now, I summon my remaining energy to position the big old box by the door of the car.'

'Brush the blasted bees off my clothes, rip off my jacket, drop me trousers too, I do, in front of a crowd or not, such is my agony.'

'Officer he take off his cape and hold it up to create a bit of a screen like. It ain't no time for the conventions of politeness I can tell you. By this time the softer parts of the body have the great old red weals nearly joined together. I know each one of those little barbed stings will have to come out later.'

'Very soon, as I lean panting and exhausted against the back of the car, the whole swarm follow the Queen's call to converge upon the box. Near collapse, I seal down the lid and request it to be delivered to my house later.'

'By this time almost every passenger has left the train to watch. Nearly the whole village has turned out to witness the event and bear testament to my humble performance.'

Ausie could contain himself no longer. 'What had the old Donga on display with no trousers on, did you?' said the exile rudely waving the front of his apron about.

'As I stumble...' Garbo paused and glared fiercely at the interjector.

'Fully dressed, and badly stung, through their massed ranks, they clap and pat me on the back, pressing coins into my swollen hands expressing their appreciation or admiration, some both.'

'I never made it home though, not under my own steam. Was flat on my back and the specialist that attended me said he counted two hundred and forty-one stings. Reckoned he had never seen anything like it in his life. Neither did the Chief Constable of Norfolk when he dropped by to see how I was and thank me.'

'Yes, sir, that's the only time I can ever remember being put flat on me back apart from times of war. How now's about that then?'

'Hardly *bee*-lievable,' commented Neville.

'Beyond *bee*-lief,' said the word wizard from Wales!

'*Bee*-buggered,' said the Concrete Kid from the big city.

Deaf Jack laughed. He had not heard a word, but he had enjoyed the actions and facial expressions though!

The Lay Preacher, 'Silly Billy', to his friends, struck up, '*All things bright and beautiful',* in the quavering dulcet tones of the hypocrites' choir. Whilst he had been listening a large notice had been attached to his back on a stiff white galley slip. Unbeknown to him, our new sandwich man marched away bearing the good word, '*Jesus Saves - but not with the Woolwich!'*

The image was somewhat spoilt as a discarded galley proof screwed into a ball the size of an orange, bounced off his bald head, and a torrent of abuse Lucifer himself would have been proud of, wended its way to heaven between the most devout strains of the hymn.

The casting machines had all stopped for some reason. Now in the background the roar of the printing perfectors from the machine room could be heard as they growled and ground out their prime produce.

CHAPTER THIRTEEN

"Romance"

As much the same way as Christmas comes once a year, Garbo used to have his old annuals. Nothing was more certain to promote a masterpiece than the yearly trip to the graves of his ancestors. Today was such a day, if only they had remembered there would have been a well arranged scarcity of ears in the immediate vicinity.

The ground had been set with an introductory tale of white bluebells in his garden. Strains from the song , 'Bluebells are blue bells, Blue bells are bluebells', hung upon the air, and he was undeterred by the common opinion that they should be called *whitebells*.

Even the hardly plausible tale of the great perch caught over the weekend had failed to hold much attention. It had been a fair try for the fishermen few.

Garbo had begun with effortless enthusiasm

'Great old fiery brute, it was, shoulders like an ox. Coloured like a clean cut jewel, with a mouth you could put a tennis ball in. Weighed damn near five clear pounds, and fought for twenty minutes like a tenacious tiger,' he called out.

Most of the crew had heard it all before, but it did contain one unusual element. There was a derivation from the home made lures of great craftsmanship.

'Drawn on to the hook he was, from within the dark waters and the weed,' he claimed with hands positioned apart in typical angler's pose. 'By a darned piece of an ordinary yellow duster.'

At times it was almost degrading to entertain the idea that he thought the crew thick enough to believe his stories. One could never quite help remembering some aspect of them, however hard they tried to forget them.

So he had arrived at the stage where something outlandish and original appeared to be required, and Garbo returned to the greater glories of good grave attendance, and proceeded to let forth. As it happened with something different.

'Nice day. Got up the churchyard we did, sometime in the late afternoon. Wife she was surprised how things had all grown up, in spite of the Spring not being too advanced this year.'

'Not me though. I keep a steady, ready, eye on all the elements. Oak before the ash. How high Moorhen, she a build her nest. All stored up in me head it is.'

'Come to the old good grave and pause a while, in remembrance and respect, to linger on times gone past. Then off to work and down to it we gets.'

'Misses she give a bit o' guidance here and there, but I carries on doing what I think is for the best.'

'Now that has a familiar ring!' said Foreman Arthur as he passed by.

Undeterred Garbo continued. 'Not long it ain't before we were down to the grass roots of the matter so to speak.'

'Took along the old sickle and scythe we had. Might be old, but still the best tools for the job I reckons. Giving it a fair old sweep I am, when the end, catch into a raised hillock. Chip straight into the fresh brown earth it did, and raise the corner of a sod.'

'Drunken bastard!' muttered the Scouser down from the keyboard for a day. The comment went unnoticed.

'Laying just to the side I see a fair sized flint. Twice, three times, the size of your fist. Bending over slow like, I remove it by tossing it some small distance away.'

Irishman interjected helpfully, 'Leaving no stone unturned, of course.'

'Straightening up we decide it's time we had a bit of a break and I rolls meself a fag. Beautiful day now, bit of sun, that still calmness that hang on the air with everything fresh, crisp and clean. Rare treat to be alive here amongst the dead.'

'Keeping me fag in me mouth, I bend over to remove yet another small stone which could impair the keen edge of the steel, when, whoop! I'm aware something has a happened!'

'Can't place it for a while. Then I hear the Wife give a little chuckle. All I can see is that somehow the ash has come off the end of my snorter on to the ground.'

'Surprisingly, I notice it is not in a position where it would have been if it had just dropped off. Sort of moved two feet away it is. There is not a breath of wind about and I cannot put the two together.'

'Turning round to the Wife I ask her what she has to laugh about, standing a there all with jollification. Then she tell me.'

'Whilst I was a leaning over, a small wee bird come and fly right in between the crook of my arm and my face. Come so close it do that it knock the ash of my darned cigarette!'

'Not surprised when she tell me though, I ain't. For I knows there's some funny things happen in the countryside. If Wife was here now I would a say to her "Now ain't that a right Gal?", She'd a say in the way that she do, "Yes, Boi, thass right, thass right it is!" softly like.'

'Howsomever. Get a thinking to my blinking self I do, and straight away conclude it's most likely to be a robin. The boldest of our British birds. Some cheeky little old cock out to get a feed.'

'Wife say she think not, and I know old Gal to be a pretty cute judge. Looking down we are aware of a faint movement on the ground. Almost like a haze it is.'

'Bending even lower, a smile come to my face, I got half the answer to the question. Dithering all around, in a million directions, is a busy colony of ants.'

'Confused, and in a pickle, they seem to be running all over each other too. Must have uncovered them, see, with the taking away of that there stone I told you about.'

'Now then, I thinks to meself. What's the bird?' The pause clearly indicated a desire for comment!

A host of suggestions came from the small crowd to assist.

'Dodo,' suggested the Australian.

'Wren,' tried the knowledgeable Northumberlander.

'How about Canary?' queried the burly unimaginative football supporter, Buster.

'House Sparrow?' ventured the Concrete Kid, who everyone agreed had probably no knowledge of other birds in his limited bricks and mortar environment.

'Bollocks!' he said rather heatedly. 'We have pigeons there as well! Loads of the bleeders, all over the place. Crapping everywhere!'

Words from the Lord's mouthpiece. 'Eat the poor things they do too. Eat anything these blasted Townies,' said the devout Lay Preacher exercising his wide knowledge on the evil ways of the sinful City dwellers, especially those that had strayed near his particular fold.

'None of 'em,' said Garbo, enthused by the unexpected level of participation.

'Settle down quiet we do and sure enough it return in a flurry of wings. None of your old cock robin is this fellow, Master.'

'No, this is a rare spotted flycatcher as plain as the eye can see. Feed so bold he do that in a little while I have him perched on a stick I'm holding in me left hand, and blast, he is eating the ants which are running up the stick held against the ground with my right one.'

'Wife she say to me that I have a fine gift with animals and all God's creatures. Great and small. Mother Nature's children the whole blessed lot of them.'

'That's right my little old Gal, I say looking at her. That's why I can look after and love you the way I do. She look at me with a softness in those ageing eyes, and she say she a love me too!'

As he leant with his hand on the case of type, grubby and original, he had a softness too, after all his eccentricities, *somebody* loved him!

This time nobody said anything and kept their heads down. The Managing Director trundled by disbelieving that the whole room could at last be working and feared the worst for another dreaded Chapel complaint in the offing.

CHAPTER FOURTEEN

Away Days

Bank Holidays normally produced some story or other, and it was quite usual for them to be based on the many events that took place over the break.

This year our good friend had been to the Oulton Broad regatta. A minor preparatory tale, to lull all into a false sense of security, had been related somewhat modestly and briefly. The saga concerned a young lad who had been rescued from certain death by drowning due solely to the quick actions of, yes, Sshsh, 'you know who'!

Any normal being would probably have dived in. Not so our valiant soothsayer and teller of wise things.

The diabolical twist decreed that a boat hook had been in reach, and adroitly brought into action. A sagging part of a sodden woolly jumper had been pierced, and the appreciative youth dragged spluttering to the shore.

If the expertise described with which the device had been wielded was true, any seasoned boatman would have been envious. The normal crowd clapping had been incorporated for the adoration of the Magi, but the audience was comparatively unmoved or appreciative in the Composing room.

Clearly this was not good enough for Garbo! He would deliver a more impressive episode. Serve up something blatantly better.

He set the scene by blowing smoke from his nostrils like a seasoned dragon.

'Not long after that we was all standing at the far end of the quay. Bit of a breeze had blown up, but still a very nice August day. Crowds had turned out in force by now, ready to enjoy themselves a rare treat.'

'Smattering of ice cream on almost every child's chubby cheeks. Others fair bulging with sweets there were. Packets of crisps being dug into.'

'Had my old eyes on a couple of fellows fishing way out towards the centre of the Broad. Could see from where we were they was catching a fair few. Nothing big like. Odd good 'un. Bream.'

'Their angling location was well over mind you. Out of the navigation channel. Obviously people like myself. With a good bit of experience on the water and in handling craft.'

'On then comes some decorated floats, garlanded with bright posies. Decked with pastel coloured wreaths in a variety of shapes and sizes. Real mass of colour some of the others. Quite brilliant and a pleasure for the eye to behold.'

'Over with that portion of the show. On to the greasy pole tricks, and rafts, you know the like. All those sort of things that makes the fun of the day.'

'Then we comes to the thing that makes the day. The thing that most people want to see. What really draws the crowd. The power boat demonstration. Great little old boats. Noisy, fast, young 'uns aboard harnessing the power of a thousand horses. Enormously powerful they sped through the water, throwing up a wash all around them that surge its way to the edge of the broad. Several we watched race down the line, prow up in the water.'

'Bit of a lull there was then, a few announcements that most could hear no detail of. If it hadn't a been for my own good hearing, I think it's fair to say none of the immediate group where we was standing, would have known what was going on.'

'Next thing, calamity, calamity! I spot out of the corner of my eye, a small boat with two persons in it, heading out towards the two anglers. As I mentioned previously, they is a fair old way out. Little old boat, it make painful progress across the water, buffeted a bit still by the returning wash. Hang about a while it does.'

'Then they come into the main tidal stream, struggle even more. Almost immediately it become abundantly clear to me what is about to happen. On the wind direction I can just about hear the hum of an engine. From experience, I know this to be the drone of a mighty powerful craft warming up.'

The Irishman meekly commented, 'Different from the drone of a swarm of bees at a level crossing then.'

'Different indeed,' replied Garbo and continued blithely.

'Casting my eyes in the appropriate direction it confirms my suspicions. Assessing the situation in an instant, I know what is to be done.'

'Tearing myself from within the very heart of the crowd, I force myself to the back. Leaving several rather startled and disgruntled people in a state of perplexity, I make my way to the adjacent flag arena.'

'Looking at the largest and tallest pole, I removes my best jacket and grip the pole with my hands. Though not so young in years as I was, it ain't long I can tell you, afore I am well towards the top. Feel the gentle wind plucking at my trousers and shirtsleeves as I make the very tip.'

'By this time, it has of course, attracted the attention of the crowd, and more eyes are upon me than ever on the regatta. This is not entirely what I am after but it helps.'

'Then, grasping the top of the flag pole between my knees, with my legs and feet entwined around it, I look towards the Control Station.'

Locking myself to the pole, I am able to make several slow movements with my arms. All but a few think I am clear out of my mind.'

Garbo stretched out his arms meaningfully in demonstration with a great seriousness.

'Not surprised. Not surprised at all,' said the FOC shaking his head in honest support.

'Then I hear what I was a waiting for. Loud and clear an announcement is made to the persons in the boat going out, to keep calm and steady. Next comes a warning to the mighty powerful craft to withhold its run, much to my relief.'

'Crikey, to my great surprise, and I must confess, my self-gratification, there follows another message.'

'Our many thanks in wholehearted appreciation to our friend up the pole, who by his semaphore message has today averted, what could have been, a very nasty accident. Thank you, Sir.'

'Giving the massed crowd below a final wave, I climb down the flag staff amidst their cheers for the second time that very day, and lose myself humbly within their packed ranks.'

'When I rejoin the Wife she can't make out where I've been,' Garbo finished his tale with a sigh.

The Brummie's voice summed it up pretty well. 'Up the bloody pole again,' it mumbled as they all departed, certainly not applauding.

Poor patient Percy shuffled his ageing worn-out white plimsolls, and waltzed away with what was left over from a nautical roll in his navy days to make alterations on the big machine.

Common knowledge has it that it is Spring which takes a young man's fancy. An old man's fancy appeared to be a lot less seasonally affected, especially in Garbo's case.

A day out knew no bounds and was as productive as any trip over the infamous marshes. The great Oulton Broad saga induced a lesser series related to Norwich, Yarmouth, wild life parks and miscellaneous out of the way places.

The sea air and salt of lazy Lowestoft appeared to be particularly stimulating.

'Knew it was going to be one of those days, the instant we caught sight of the policeman controlling the traffic, on the way into the town. Holding it up, letting the cars filter in a bit at a time. All very reasonable.'

'Come to our turn and a grin started to form on my face. Wife she want to know what I am smiling about. I tells her to wait and see.'

An irreverent Australian accent enquired, 'Not farted again old Cobber, had you?'

The rather rude interruption was totally ignored as Garbo continued.

'As we draws level with the Officer, I winds down the window. From the position I was a sitting of, in the passenger seat, behind the driver, I call out in a friendly way. "Can you tell me the way to St Nazarre please?" hand to mouth.'

'Policeman look a bit startled at first, then his face wreath in smiles and his hand is stretched out in welcome. He say I haven't changed a bit in thirty years, but now how come I recognise him, as he knows he isn't what he used to be.'

With a grin I gestulate, gesticulate, his medal ribbons. Secret's there okay. I knew there was only a handful of us mentioned in despatches for that particular ribbon. Far fewer were well over six feet three inches tall like this fine fellow. Even less came from East Anglia. Give that to my exceptional memory for a face, once seen and never forgotten, and we are home and dry.'

'Traffic seemed to be piling up behind us now so he let's us go, with a promise of a beer in a tavern just outside of town in the evening.'

'Proceeding towards the town a little further, I am amazed to see a blur of colour in front of us. We are approaching the swing bridge, and it seems as though either part of it has been painted red, or it's spattered and streaked with blood. Can hardly believe my eyes.'

'I hadn't said much, but as soon as we are on to the bridge I takes a closer look.'

'Daughter in-law, she say they are a painting of the bridge. I saw they were not. Son, he side with his wife of course and a rare argument start up. Even the Wife think it is paint. All disagree with poor old Dad like.'

'Shame on them,' said the sympathetic Lay Preacher man in a rare display of jest.

'It's an upside down world and full of injustices,' said Aussie laughing loudly.

Garbo appeared grateful and continued. 'Not being quite as old and stupid as they think, I state there is only one way to solve the argument. Stop the car! All get out and have a good old look. More fuss. Women don't want to stop. I feels like swearing. Son, he say nowt.'

'Bit reluctant he is, until I force upon the door and almost leap out. Grind to a halt we do, and the Boy, he is something riled. Embarrassed too about all the fuss and having to brake hard causing the chap behind to sound off his horn.'

'Now I can see quite clearly though. Crossing the pavement to the reddened rails I gently run my hand through the mass of coloured streaks.'

'Wife holler out that I will get the paint all over me best clothes. Then the rest of the sentence die on her lips and they all gasp with surprise.'

'Hold out my hand with an invitation to inspect their darned paint, and note that they are wrong. The surface of my hand has become alive.'

'Clustered together, *like paint*. Blast I'll give you that, are about a hundred brightly coloured ladybirds. Bishebarnabees.'

'It is now clear to them the cause of the colouring. No one apologises. I push the Boy's head forward and ask him if he still think his father is still a silly old bugger. Blast, he don't say a word for the next hour.'

'Anyway, we park up the car, after a bit more of a fuss and me having to give directions for the final manoeuvrings as it were. Pay the fee I does, and introduce myself to the attendant asking him to keep a personal eye on the vehicle as it is special model. Has particular modifications the normal person may not see which we have carried out.'

'Jesus wept,' said Doncaster Don, 'you are not going to tell us you sent the car to Sweden for them are you?'

'Indeed not. In a few quick strides I soon catch up with the rest of the party, who had trounced off while I was a talking.'

There were many present who knew exactly how they felt and saw it as quite understandable!

'Then we come to what we had made the trip for. Son, he had been none too keen for me to see his best friend's shipyard where he work. Taken a fair bit of talking into, but he had eventually relented. Always been interested in the construction of things I have, yes, especially those made by hand. It's the Craftsman element in us all I suppose Comrades.'

'Spoke to several of the carpenters there and saw a variety of designs in their various stages of construction. Was able to discuss at length some of the finer points in boat building and offer some suggestions, which the top management, I might add, said could prove useful.'

'In fact one of the workers did say as we were about to leave the department, "When you a taking over Guvnor?" Amused the Boy and his Wife that did. Then we gets to the final stages. The finishing off and the actual testing on the water.'

'Outside we were by this time, on a nice little quay. Small, sea-going craft was about to be launched down the miniature slipway. Course my eye travel to the water, before the ship actually strike the surface. Much to my surprise there is an abundance of life there. Near towards the middle is a bunch and mass of white fully fledged swans. Know at a glance they are Hoopers.'

'What, they make a sort of *Oop-ooping* noise do they?' asked the inquisitive Concrete Kid.

'No,' replied Garbo tritely. 'They build their nests in children's' hoops if they see them laying around,' and continued with a knowing smile.

'Once craft hits the water and travels on it, a great bow wave is sent surging across the surface. Old swans they take to the air with a great commotion and flapping. In no time at all they are in a formation and circling over to return to their watery residence.'

'I tells the Manager there is forty-three of them. He look at me something surprised and say they have been trying to count them every day for a year and never get the total right the first time. Some times they end up counting them five times. Do it for the records they been asked to keep. He knows I'm right because they had only confirmed the exact number a quarter of an hour before.'

'He ask me how I know. I just wink at him and tell him to put it down to experience.'

'When we come to go he's still a puzzled over it. I just keep on smiling and saying nothing.'

'A time we get into the car it has become quite infectious. All the family want to know how on earth I could be so precise. Well, I won't tell them. Keep them guessing. Right until we gets in the pub in the evening. Then I tells them.'

'See every old swan, it empty its bowels just once a day. Right near where we was standing was the muckiest pile you could want to see. Swan's droppings everywhere in little heaps. I had just totted up the number of fresh ones for the amount of birds in residence, and Bob's your uncle, an answer we have ourselves.'

'Mind you I could have told him to raise his eyes to the sky and count the blighters after he frightened them off the water every day. Why, say I, make things too bloomin' simple for people though. Eh?' he queried the diminishing audience who hardly heard the parable for the end of the day.

'Especially,' he added with an unusual venom, 'if they been a referring to you as a bloody old fool all day!'

'Anyways, blast me, if all that wasn't blinking enough, the damn curtains in the Pub caught light in the evening and we topped off the day with a rare good performance to put them out, old copper and I.'

'A right couple of bright sparks', said Sussex Sam.

'Landlord, he was something grateful to us, I can tell you, Garbo rejoined.'

'Didn't get another round of applause from those present did you?' asked Skipton's special son.

The listeners quickly dispersed grateful for the extremely educational experience relating to the toilet habits of the royal bird, and wondering upon the colour and freshness of swan droppings. Perhaps there would be a chemical or scientific paper produced by Professor R. Gray, they wondered, but doubted so.

Garbo picked up the bonus slip left on his frame. He noted the poor payment, marched to the FOC and vented his discontent.

'Rubbish and an insult to our Craft this scheme, for a good day's work Mr FOC,' he fumed.

'Indeed brother, indeed. My point exactly! Get seven signatures and we'll have a meeting about it,' said the Father ready to cash in on any opportunity for an affray.

CHAPTER FIFTEEN

A Sticky Customer

It was one of those warm sultry country days which remain in the memory even several summers later. The afternoon was somewhat spoilt by having to take the bodies off, and to within, the dark doors of the factory.

The drab of the black and the white was obviously too much for our mutual Friend on such a day. Garbo had made a couple of half-hearted attempts at raising interest in two low quality luke warm wonders, but had received only the absolute minimum of appreciation and enthusiasm.

Obviously determined to have his hearing of the day, he descended upon the small knot of the brotherhood, gathered in a queue to take a cold drink from the vending machine, and a little conversation to go with it.

Garbo seized the opportunity and successfully cornered a captive audience, and leant against the cool steel imposition stone on one elbow. In the starting mode he pulled away in first gear.

'Well blowed if I didn't see something on the way home to dinner that didn't half make me smile,' he commenced with a broad grin.

'Just calling in at the butcher's shop on the hill, when my attention was attracted by a very attractive young woman. It was very apparently she was in some minor state of distress or surprise.'

The Australian stroked his brown beard slowly and contributed thoughtfully, 'I hope this is not going to be a story of lust and depravity,' he said seriously.

Garbo removed the soggy end of the cigarette from his lips, spat upon the floor, and continued.

'In a quick stride or two, I was at her side, grasping her elbow and showing her my small reassurance.'

'What did I tell you, he's got his willy out already,' whispered Aussie invoking a few titters.

The tale was continued, the comment unheard or ignored.

'With a smile I looks into her face and ask her what has put her in such a tizz on such a fine day. She recognised me straight away. Mind you I reckons I know most of the faces around these parts. What is more, I tell you that if I see a strange face around here, I'll remember it, and, it not be afore long, when I finds out who they are and where's they a come from! Yes, master.'

There was no doubt whatsoever that all of the latent listeners believed that bit!

'Pretty pleased to see a friendly face she was, and held out her shopping basket to me quite aghast.'

'She being the wife of one of those people from *away*, that keeps appearing round here these days, I ain't ever surprised at what I see and hear now from people.'

Garbo cast his eyes around the room fixing it upon one or two of the latest arrivals who were turning out to be very poor listeners.

'She tell me her shopping basket has surely come alive. Positive she is that she has seen the wicker work move. Asks me to take a look for myself.'

'Taking the old basket from her, and holding it just a foot from above the ground I gives it a little gentle, but firm mark you, shake. Repeating this several times there appeared to be no startling results.'

The movement was acted out with great aplomb.

'But in here,' Garbo said, tapping the side of his greying bald head with a gnarled and grubby finger, 'the old brain box is a working overtime. Ticking away to come up with a fair conclusion.'

'Place the basket on the ground, very gently, and sit down on the kerb and remove one of my shoes.'

To those acquainted with the smell of his feet on a hot day, it was a small wonder the young woman had not passed out or run away! It was also believable that the small crowd he was now claiming had assembled. They may have been drawn by the need to trace a foul smell.

'Got me shoe I have, and takes up the basket in one hand to hold it about a foot above the ground again. With a little deft judgement I give the basket a smart rap with the heel of my shoe.'

'There is a gasp of amazement, from the young woman, and several among the audience, as it appears to them I have knocked some small pieces off the basket.'

'Picks up the little inch and a half long things from the ground, and place them on the outstretched palm of my hand for her to see.'

'As they start to move slowly in my hand, as if by magic or miracle, I am able to answer the question from the crowd.'

'Yes, my friends. I am able to tell them these are just humble stick insects. Another one of our munificent Mother Nature's wonders. Something relieved is the young woman, to know her sanity is secure.'

'People want to know how on earth they ever got there, and my mind's been back to when I was a boy, yes it has. When we used to keep these little critters in a match box and cart them about everywhere with us.'

'When we come into town one day with Aunty, she have a particular shop in mind to go to, we hang around at the door declining to go in. Out come the thing of the moment. You've guessed it,' Garbo gleamed noting the wry smile on a victim's face.

'The stick insects! Used to put them on the door posts and leave the little old blighters to see how long they could hang on to the shiny bits of the door posts. Young buggers.'

With an unusual simplicity of the whole truth Garbo announced, 'Well, of course I am not going to tell you that these are some of the ones I left behind all those years ago. Might be their great, great, grandfathers though I suppose.'

'Oh no, we wouldn't believe that. Not at all,' said Alan the Essex exile, incredulously, with a cheeky grin.

'But the craze comes back,' Garbo continued. 'These could have either dropped into the basket from such a place, or some young devil popped them in for a trick deliberately. Got a fair funny sense of humour, and ingenuity, has the good little old country lad. Bless every one of them I say! Not like his unimaginative comparators from the town!'

The conclusion was thrown with a scathing look at the Concrete Kid, who felt extremely offended as he was a regular listener if nothing else. He replied with his stock answer to many things. 'Bollocks!'

'That's right,' said Brummie, 'they are all too busy playing with their bollocks and masturbating, over dirty books and things, popping pills, in those shitty city sort of places,' delivering a hearty poke in the ribs in good fun to the Cockney.

'Right, Cobber. They are all wankers in this God forsaken hell hole of yours. You wanna get out where it's really hot. See some real varmints,' said Aussie positively insulting everyone who was present.

'Well, I think it's been very *SSSSticky*, today,' said Foxy as he departed, adjusting his spectacles for the fiftieth time of the day.

'Silly *Basket*,' muttered Herbert as he crammed sorts into his composing stick with the speed of sound. The consumption of eight pints of good ale during the dinner hour done wonders for his performance.

'Really *wood-n-t*, have believed it,' said apprentice boy with the nice voice. Usually he was a lad prepared to believe anything. Some thought he was a boy who would go far. Others thought the sooner and further he went the better.

Solly sighed and slipped the leads between the lines aware that escape from the East Anglian doom was now only a remote possibility. He wished he had never read the advert pages of the *Journal*. Trapped for a life sentence, chained to the frame, in madness with morons, far from his beloved bright lights and busy streets.

But then, with Caslon Old Face for a friend, who could go wrong?

PURSESTRING PEOPLE

The ones who are mean, and the ones who are tight,
will pinch up their purses and hide from the light,
with copper and silver, and pound notes galore,
just credit bank balance, by depositing more.
A miser become, with possessions so dear,
a medium to push, away friends who come near.
It's pride of a place, in a world of their own,
where some greedy seed, flowers, so easily sown.
To cheat and defraud in devious ways,
the friends in your life, for the rest of their days!

Three cheers for the Bonus Scheme!

CHAPTER SIXTEEN

Turning a Blind Eye

The hot weather continued, week after week the sun shone and drought approached. For many this induced a sleepiness and laid back approach, shedding what clothes they could. The Australian rolled up in his shorts and became the subject of much jest and ribaldry from his colleagues. Garbo of course was affected differently.

Whilst everyone else sweltered in the minimum of apparel, the Soothsayer remained coolly clad in the ash-smothered waistcoat, with his eyes on fire as usual.

Truly his appearance was heralded by a stronger than usual body odour, but most people still put it down to the ancient woollen army socks he was so proud of. In accordance with custom and practice, Garbo would no doubt have had some deeper reason for his state.

A hitherto undiagnosed disease, or the remains of an unusual health giving property, deviously obtained on some distant, far flung shore, would have been on the cards, but no one ever mentioned it to him. They preferred to suffer in silence, as rare as it ever was. Consequently when the factory filled with the dismal and depressed faces, there was one person waiting to cheer on the day. Not many minutes passed before Garbo was ready to address the ensemble.

'Damn funny thing how this hot weather affect the creatures, though they be better equipped than us for all the seasons,' was his opening parody.

There was little resistance on such a sweltering day to the ominous and inevitable tale. The honourable few of the Companionship gave in easily.

'Got home this dinner time, and there was the Wife waiting to greet me with a fresh cold salad. Most of which come out of the garden of course. When old dog she start to make a bit of a shimozzle.'

'Not barking mind you. No, she's a quiet sort of a dog, and been trained different from that, as I've a told you all before. Shaking her head, and blowing down her darn nose she is. Rubbing her ear with her paw and giving those long yawny groans. Keep putting her head on one side, then t'other.'

'Now, I say to myself, little old girl she's a trying to say something to me. Tell me something. So off we follows her round to the back door step.'

'Well there she is, bless my soul, cavorting around, found something she's rare proud of. Smooth shiny object coiled up in a heap.'

'I say to the Missus it is a good old grass snake come out for a sunning. Mind you it seemed kind of funny to me that it hadn't moved at all.'

'Knowing quite a bit about all sorts of creatures that I do, the first job is to put the dog out of the way. Wife soon keep her quiet in the kitchen with a great old bone I snaffled from the slaughter house, at the weekend, when I took a brace of hares up to them.'

'Slow like, I cut a forked stick from the hedge, by the compost heap, and move to within about two feet of the reptile and crouch down.'

Garbo crouched to the floor with a sidestick in his hand ready to perform the act to be described.

'Didn't want to give it a tune then?' commented the long-haired lad learning the guitar.

'Nope,' affirmed Garbo. 'Started to tickle the old snake with the end of the stick just by its throat. Meanwhile I talks to it in low voice, in a very soft way. Soon old snake is so docile I can pick it up and caress it freely.'

'Mind you, what a size it was, she be thirty-six inches long I know, which must be something of a record for these parts I should imagine.'

'Bless my poor old soul, when I looks closer it can be seen the poor blighter is not quite to rights. Blind in one eye it is.'

'Then my mind goes back to the days when our eldest lad was just a mischievous and curious young 'un. Not like the great hulking brute of a fireman he is these days in his uniform.'

'Kept us awake one summer, damn near every night he did, a moaning and a feared that an eye he see kept watching him, while he play with his little old cars on the back door step.'

'Putting two and two together is not always easy with a child, but I can remember going out to the step with the lad to see what all the trouble is about.'

'*Eye-eye*, what's all this about, constable?' an alien voice piped up from somewhere under a frame.

'There sure enough, under the step he say, is the eye he keep on saying is a looking at him. Rubbish, I think to myself, I can't see a blooming thing. Howsomever, cuts a longish thin stick from the bush, put point on it, and poke it sharply in the crevice under the step. I tell him that it will all be okay now.'

'Blast, much to my surprise a blinking grass snake come sliding out and vanish into the hedgerow, shaking its head.'

'Now then. When I puts this snake down, dinner time, it turn and look at me. Slow, mean, and almost vengeful, though a grass snake be a harmless creature.'

'Watch in silence for a while I do and feel some sort of remorse for that cold-blooded slitherer. See it's obvious to me that all those years ago it was me that robbed this very snake of the sight in one of its eyes. Yes, all those years ago, when I poked that sharp stick into the hole. Yes, Master. Time is a funny old thing.'

Andrew made one of his rare 'Fleeting', contributions, 'Turn a *blind-eye* to it I expect it did, with no hard feelings,' he said ripping off somewhere or other to take the pee out of someone else.

Garbo nearly managed to get a double dose off the ground but was halted in the early stages.

'Mind you, I can tell you far odder tales than that of lame and disfigured animals and birds,' he started.

'Once there was the time when I shot a pigeon with three eyes so I did. Had another eye set in the back of its head!'

Yorkie headed it off instantly. 'Only surprise to me is that it wasn't up its arsehole and flying backwards when you shot it,' he said with exasperation.

Garbo was not amused and there was worse to come.

'Reminds me of how they catch elephants in the Congo,' grated the Cockney, laughing. 'They put a line of peas on a path that leads to a bleedin' great hole in the ground.'

'Aha!' whooped Garbo, his twinkly eyes immediately interested. 'Cunning eh!' he started.

'Yes,' replied the Londoner. 'When the elephant wants a *pee* it follows the trail and then falls in the hole!'

'That, was a *piss-poor* joke,' quipped the Deputy Foc.

Garbo, not lost for words on any occasion, had the last ones.

'You can always tell a Londoner,' he said with a fearsome glare, 'but you can't tell him much!'

High hoots of derision dented the depression.

Hands thrust deep in the capacious pockets of the grubby apron, Garbo stumped grumpily off to the bog.

The old cottages next door to the factory were being pulled down to make a car park. Caught up in the ravages of the march of time, dust flew and the clay lump, sprouting spiky lumps of straw crashed into an untidy heap.

With the demolition of the cottage, a few mice had sought refuge in the modern confines of the factory but were soon eradicated.

Arriving back from dinner, Garbo raised his head high into the air and stopped dead in his tracks.

'Blast if I don't smell a rat. Old house rat too. Don't smell like none of your farm fellows.'

It was remarkable the encrusted nostrils could smell anything other than the snuff. As if to discredit the unspoken word, the bakelite box was produced and a couple of sharp taps administered. The worn lid was raised and a pinch laid on the back of the hand. Within a few seconds those in the vicinity could notice it in the air too.

Getting down on all fours, Garbo proceeded to unload the piles of coffee stained proofs and treasures residing under the frame. The room was roused with a trumpet of triumph as Garbo announced the invaders had been at his personal supply of sugar lumps in the tatty cardboard box.

'Not rats mate,' said the Concrete Kid, 'it's just three blind mice.'

Several dirts were produced by excited Garbo as proof, and a delivery on the values of our danger to hepatitis and *'Veill's'* disease were delivered. Fear not, our protector would vent his genius upon the evil creature's entrapment we were assured.

Three hours later a contraption had been erected. It truly cost a small fortune in production time. Sheer cunning determined its placement by the door with the hole in it. A conglomeration of string from parcels, page cord, and a stripped length of electrical wire were all putty in the hands of the master.

Four lengths of leaden mounting material were ominously suspended like the sword of Damocles over the hole, and two side sticks and a four page imposition chase diabolically drawn together with more string.

The final flourish touch, compiled with great neatness, was the small patch of sugar placed on the floor. Craftsman made, of course!

A deep detailed explanation of the construction was defeated by the time's up bell for home and the general exodus. The impressed colleagues would all wait in eager anticipation for the morrow.

Next morning Garbo was among the first to arrive. One and all were welcomed with great guffaws of glee to the killing area. Success had indeed been achieved.

The assassination complete. But - of course in a *very, very* unusual way.

There swinging six feet in the air hung the dead and departed demon. Poor devil had never reached the sugar, but tripped into the tiniest of snares. Or so he said. There were uncharitable persons who suggested he had brought the huge brown rat in with him! The strangest quirk was, it *also* only had one good eye. The other looked like an old healed injury, and induced much jest as to why it walked into the snare.

Yorkie claimed it had its address on a note tucked in its rectum. A change from his normal claim of a birth certificate so it knew how old it was!

Robbo the bobbo produced another of his witless puns and said, 'thereby hangs *'a tail'*.

The Lay Preacher, who in his normal unbelieving way, claimed he thought he saw it move, was told by the Londoner that might be the case, but if so it is because *'it's snarely dead!'*

The staff all suffered and maintained their own silence as the full field was commanded with lucid descriptions of trappings extolling exaggerated equal successes in all corners of the globe.

Big ones, small ones, stupid ones. Ones of intelligence and character. Black, brown, white, black and white, he had caught them all. They were sure he had? Or were they? What a start to the day!

The light swung, shadowless shimmers bounced back from the shiny inkless quads and spaces of the type. The cases displayed their silvery contents for consideration.

Furniture laid piled upon the cold harsh, unwelcoming stones beside sleeping pages. A few wooden picas lay ink-stained and oily as a stubborn tribute to the past. A collection of Cornerstone quoins, looking virginally new and without work stains, exhibited themselves as a demonstration of the decade's new technology!

The hum of the perfectors hung now unheard in the background. The monotype casters with their incessant noise, threatened the same sanity Talbot Lanston had lost when he invented them a half century before.

Was all print madness? Could this mirror image that each day made right read wrong and wrong read right as a natural performance upon its leaden face, be security?

Did headlines scream from newspapers, and make news to impact upon wild world markets, mice and men, changing fortunes and fostering fears tuned and pruned by the printer's hand?

Was this the word and medium of learning?

> *Nay, 'twas but a way to earn a crust.*
> *Something solid we all could trust!*

A job for life!.

How wrong we were all to be!

THE EPITAPH

Like all material and physical substances, time and wear take their toll. Similar to an oak-aged claret, Garbo and all of his associated era, had arrived at uncorking time. Sixty-five long years of an almost unchanging, unchallenged era could not be staved off by the emerging nineteen-eighties. Not by tales tall, or by tales small. Not by closed shop, cunning, nor by Craft.

The last day of work hung heavy on the air for Garbo as it has done for many who have seen their skills become redundant. The preceding month been a lonely, long, sad, and difficult time as he and they have watched the love of their work and craftsmanship slipping away, like all those of an enforced departure in today's ruthless money-motivated world.

Many may wonder how his poor long-suffering wife would have managed under such an incessant barrage of narrative. Experience was on her side. Now there was a lady with a story to tell!

With great care the final daily docket was calculated to produce a low bonus. Craft and quality could now not be squandered at any price. Precision and painstaking accuracy could not, and would not, be sold in exchange for the be-littling of Garbo's skills, or that of the noble companions within *the* Industry.

Unmotivated by financial greed the principles held firm. 'A job must be done, and done well.' Nothing should become an exclusion to the world of dreams. The invasion of Craft an intrusive insult, slander upon the epitome of natural skill and tradition!

Material values and pastimes took on an Oscar Wilde profile, 'the price of everything and the value of nothing', for Garbo and many like him in their own orbits. Economic theory was individual excellence dominant over shoddy quick jobs. Objective market were forces faced out by subjective human values.

The world of Craft was going out of the door with Garbo, and all his contemporaries across the Country. The '*Times*' they were a changing, without consultation or democracy!

Filmsetting placed its negative influences on positive skills. Knowledge evilly fed upon itself, self-generating acceleration, creating computer images plied upon paper.

New stars rose as the old moon fell. Suns set, but failed to rise with vigour, colour and warmth on the morrow.

Technology's coldness froze out the true spirit of the 'Companionship', and the warmth of loyalties and friendships forged. Lead, tin and antimony, became as devalued as gold, frankincense and myrrh.

What did and does remain?

Something still, and of great importance!

That *Chapel!*

The closeness of the Industry has moved away as apprenticeships have declined and cold metal cabinets housing computers become the love of those in white coats replacing the canny compositor and his little metal letters.

Perhaps Lord Alfred Tennyson's words can say something to us about our position as we move into the next century and leave much of our strengths and understanding behind us. Words for troubled travellers tossed about in the turbulence of time.

They are the same as chosen for the final National Graphical Association conference from the rostrum in tribute to the 'Chapel' as delivered then:

"We are not now that strength which in old days
Moved earth and heaven; that which we are, we are;
One equal temper of heroic hearts,
Made weak by time and fate, but strong in will
To strive, to seek, to find, but not to yield!"

Garbo and a lot of his traditionally type-cast fellows have clung on to strive, and proudly fight in the face of adversity. On the streets of Warrington and Wapping they lifted our spirits with them in the final desperate struggles, shoulder to shoulder, still in that durable *Companionship*. Recognising at times the inevitability of defeat, but with a determined pride and stubbornness resisting until the bitter end.

When we look back, not in anger always, at that lost power and privilege, there is much of mirth and merriment to remember.

Time, in spite of all this, will hold firm those memories of an era past. The laughter and the smiles.

Our industry's great eccentrics and characters along with its idiosyncrasies and oddities. Unique! For that is what it was, and still is, whatever its shape today, *"Our Industry"*.

No doubt the great composing room in the sky is receiving a very special share of charisma and individuality. Goodbye to all those many comps and connivers, and Garbo's. . .*'The Great!'*

Me, my ending is different! As a Compositor in the seventies I saw it along the lines of the verse written then:

I've tried to be first, but not often won,
in various assortments of races I've run.
Perhaps if I look, and examine it close,
my pattern for life has been far too morose.
My work on my back, had become a great weight,
method and change a subject of hate.
So, what will become, when the end draweth near?
A pat on the back, a pitiful cheer?
Or, perhaps it will end, with a sardonic laugh,
on my tombstone enamelled one quaint epitaph -

"D. Gladwell. . .also ran. . ."

These days I see it differently, no regrets, but the deepest of sympathies to all those for whom things did not turn out so well as they did for me!

GLOSSARY

Hopefully an assembly of helpful printing terms for the out of trade person and the otherwise interested party

Bodkin: Pointed awl (sometimes called a Bradall in other industries) used to tuck in cords that tied the page together, lifting lines for correction, pushing down spaces between words, and a host of minor misappropriations. Pear-shaped wooden handle and the thin metal spike around three inches long (see illustration page 100).

Case: See page 160 for layout. Odd display lines and correction characters selected from the wooden trays. Contained all characters and punctuation signs, but most important the:
Em and En: Printing measurement system. Six *ems* equal one inch. Two *En's* equal one *Em*. Seventy two points equal one *Em* and therefore 12 points. The term *Pica,* is also based on the standard *Em* for old time measurement. The *m* as a space width was also termed as a *Mutton*. Rotated around width of the lower case 12pt m character. 0.166044" the key measurement. The *Em* also had an 18-unit set width division within each font size. Widths and lengths were determined in numbers of pica (12pt) En's for furniture and text widths or lengths. Each type body size would have its own *Em* in body width being determined by the character width of its own lower case m as far as internal spacing was concerned.

Chapel: The method of organisation for in-house groups of workers to a trade union co-ordinate. Usually three or more employees, excluding Management. Based on the first printers being in Caxton's Chapel Press and in Churches. World wide industry name also used in Journalistic areas, not necessarily trade union orientated. May also be termed as *'The Companionship'*. Joseph Moxon mentions it in his works *The Mechanick Exercise* of 1638. Spelt at that time 'Chappel' and can be traced in the *Combinations Act*.

Father of the Chapel, FOC; Foc: Normally annually elected leader of the Chapel in the department, trade section, of the workplace. In 1648, again, recorded by Joseph Moxon, in those days, as being the oldest man in the print shop. Versatile trouble-maker, peacemaker, panacea for all evils, speaker of wise and foolhardy words at times! Workers' grassroot representative on the shopfloor who has links to Branch offices of the said Union and enacts main Union policies directly upon the members. Maintainer of Union discipline and practices via his *Committee*. An *MOC* can also exist as Mother of the Chapel.

Forme: Collection of pages, having been placed on a stone, locked by quoins into a metal surround, a chase, capable of being conveyed to the letterpress printing machine. Usually in numbers divisible by four. e.g. 8. 16, 32, 64 pages, but can be 1 or 2 pages. Very heavy in the larger sizes, and often conveyed upright on a pair of narrow wheels whilst resting in an inch wide gulley a foot or so long. The larger book forme was positioned on and printed from the sliding bed of a press or letterpress printing machine.

Furniture: Wood or metal of varying lengths and widths (of ems), which are placed between pages to keep the type apart in the locking up process, and to dictate the margins around the edge of a page in a book etc., termed *heads, tails, gutters, foredges, backs.*

Frame: The Compositor's work bench with an angled top and sloping surface for placing cases of type and galleys to work on. Cases were also stored horizontally in racks in the frame. Made of wood or latterly metal. Five feet high and around two case-lengths long to six feet in length. Often assembled longways end-on to make a *random*.

Galley: Originally made of wood but latterly thin metal tray approximately 30" long, and 6" wide. The depth a little less than the type height (approximately fifteen sixteenths of an inch), with thin, turned up sides, and at back end, used for keeping pages on. Corrections to pages were made on galley in the earlier stages of production and type cast directly upon it from the casting machines. Pages were stored, then slid, tied up, from this onto the stones for next stage. Other sizes available.

Letterpress: System of printing by direct impression from raised surface. The sheet of paper passed between the rotating cylinder and a moveable flat bed but rotary presses produced copies via great reels of paper. The German Koenig credited with first steam driven press in 1814.

Linotype: Composing machine which cast letters into a solid line, a slug, to be assembled as a page. Used for paperback book production and principally in the newspaper industry. Different keyboard lay from the Qwerty arrangement for fingering. Keys arranged in similar order to the lay of the case. Invented by Ottmar Merganthaler, (another darned Hun, as Garbo could have said), in 1866.

Monotype: Individual type or typecasting machine, creating the formulation of single characters by the process of a great deal of noise and molten metal. Talbert Lanston credited with the invention in 1887 and came on the market in 1897 eradicating the jobs of hundreds of case hands who formerly set by hand. Ran in tandem with a mechanical keyboard with Qwerty layout which punched holes in a spool of paper the approximate size of a toilet roll. The Casting machine blew air throughout these round perforated holes which in turn moved a set of brass matrixes around to cast the metal letters individually.

Perfector: Large letterpress printing machine. A veritable monster capable of printing on both sides of the sheet of paper in one pass through the cylinders, usually from two separate beds containing formes.

Pye or Pie: The unfortunate incidence of assembled type sorts in a page, or line, being rendered apart into a disorganised format or heap from lack of care or accident. A minor disaster if this was a foreign language and often required resetting as opposed to reassembly by fingers, into original format.

Quoin: Metal screw function, or wood wedge device around 1.5 inches in length, and less than type height, used to tighten type in place by tapping tight with mallet and shooter, or turning key clockwise. Hempel with a two part serrated wedge. Cornerstone,

Wickersham with revolving cams on a screw thread base, are various metal designs.

Sidestick: Long gradually wedge shaped piece of wood, tapering from approximately one inch, down to half an inch over its thirty inch length. Used upon galleys (and in older style formes a shorter page-length) of type in conjunction with wooden Quions and type to be locked firmly in position. The coins were loosened on the galley stick for carrying out corrections to type on a galley.

Stone: Generally large steel table top up to 4" thick, set on an iron framework used to lay pages of type upon in order to lock them up into a group for printing (imposition). Got exceptionally cold in the winter months but a good focal point for conversation and Union Chapel meetings. Part of the *Imposing* or *Imposition Ship,* where there would be up to thirty workers in a room in a typical large bookhouse. Took its name from old lithographic oil stones from which prints were produced.

Type and its height: Whilst Johaan Gutenburg, printer of Mainz, Germany, is widely credited with the invention of moveable type used in his 42-line bible in the mid fifteenth century, that may not be totally correct. In AD 1049, a Chinaman, Pi Sheng, developed a method of producing separate baked clay characters capable of being rearranged to form a page. Precise height of a printing character 0.9195 inch, 0.918 for display faces. Made from a composition of mainly lead with around 6-10% tin and the 20-30% variation of antimony, sometimes 2-5% copper or nickel for hardness. Had a horizontal niche (nick) in the front side to determine correct way round particularly for b, d, p, q. One time sized by names: *pearl, ruby, nonpariel, brevier, bourgeois, long primer,* and others.

Type faces: Range of designs cut into the formation of an alphabet (a *font*) with distinguishing characters. Serif and sans serif are the most easily defined comparison. Comparable example: by Eric Gill, his **sans serif** (Gill) used on underground signs in London, and Times New Roman (as this face) the cut for the *Times* newspaper remaining today in that publication. A range of over a thousand was available in hot metal form, and in large wood letters many ancient cuts lasted out to the end of the days. Had serial numbers such as *Times 327; Plantin 110; Caslon Old Face 128*.

Unions: The old compositor's and letterpress machine minder's unions were the Typographical Association and the London Typographical Society which merged to form the NGA = National Graphical Association, craft printing union. Eventually merging in 1982 with other printing unions: ASLP (Lithoprinters and platepreparers); ACP (Readers in the Associated Correctors of the Press). T&E (Telegraphists); SLADE (Lithographic Artists, Designers & Engravers and process workers); E&S (Electrotypers and Stereotypers) and finally NUWDAT (Wallpaper workers). Today these are merged with SOGAT 92 to form the GPMU (Graphical Paper & Media Union), a large and influential craft and non craft Union.

The Devil's Bed - The Case Lay - on a good day!